"Why couldn't you have trusted me?"

David asked the question, his eyes like cold steel. I said incoherently, "Please. Please don't say it. I can't bear—"

I heard him sigh, and then he gripped my arm. "Lucy," he said in a queer, shaky voice. "Don't! You mustn't cry. I can't bear it, either. Stop it—do you hear?"

He pressed my wet face hard against his shoulder and shook me gently. And then he took my cap off and put it down carefully on the table, and ran his long fingers into my hair, and I heard a strange little laugh before he put his mouth on mine.

After what seemed a long time he moved his lips to my ear.

"I'm sorry," he said. "I had to stop you."

Great love stories never grow old...

And we at Harlequin are proud to welcome you, our readers, to HARLEQUIN CLASSIC LIBRARY—a prime selection of time-tested, enduring favorites from the early lists of Harlequin's best-selling Romances.

Harlequin Romances have been read throughout the world for many years. Why? There are as many reasons as there are people. But longtime readers tell us that our books combine the enjoyment of travel, the intrigue of good plots, warm and interesting characters and the thrill of love. Each novel possesses an emotional appeal that sweeps you right into the wonderful world of romance!

As publishers of Harlequin Romances, we take a great deal of pride in our books. Since 1949 Harlequin has built its reputation on the solid base of quality and originality. And now our widely popular paperback romance novels have been translated into eighteen languages and are sold in more than eighty countries.

So...if you relish a classic love story, one whose appeal has lost nothing over the years, read the timeless Harlequin Romances in the HARLEQUIN CLASSIC LIBRARY. We hope you enjoy this story and all the others in our special selection of beautiful love stories from years past.

For a free catalogue of the books available, write to:
HARLEQUIN READER SERVICE
(In the U.S.) M.P.O. Box 707, Niagara Falls, N.Y. 14302
(In Canada) Stratford, Ontario, Canada   N5A 6W2

Nurse Elliot's Diary

KATE NORWAY

Originally published as Harlequin Romance # 525

HARLEQUIN
CLASSIC LIBRARY

TORONTO • LONDON • LOS ANGELES • AMSTERDAM
SYDNEY • HAMBURG • PARIS • STOCKHOLM • ATHENS • TOKYO

Original hardcover edition published by
Mills & Boon Limited 1960
ISBN 0-373-80025-8

Harlequin edition first published June 1960
Golden Harlequin Library edition, Volume XXIX, published September 1972
Harlequin Classic Library edition published June 1980

Printed in Canada

CHAPTER ONE

THIS AFTERNOON we signed our agreements in matron's office, and she smiled tigerishly and said, "I hope you three now feel that you really belong here."

We murmured nervously that we did, but I think we have been trying ever since to persuade ourselves that it was true. Everything seems to have happened so quickly, lately.

When Peta stood at my door half an hour ago, saying good-night, she looked around the room with one pointed eyebrow lifted and the corners of her mouth twitching. "Well, I suppose we can settle down to the notion that this is home, now. Now that we've signed on. Fine for me, after that ghastly hostel. Must be a bit of a shaker for you, though, coming from The Laurels, isn't it?"

I shook my head emphatically. "Not nearly so drafty! Father says he's finding the apartment so cozy that he can't think why he didn't sell the house before. And here was I, thinking he'd be heartbroken! Just shows—people don't run true to form, do they?"

"Well, did *we*?"

"Of course we did. But the people at the bank probably don't think so. 'Two such promising girls,' as Mr. Hyde said!"

Peta's eyes crinkled. "Yes, the old hypocrite. I darned near asked him to put it in writing."

She waved her hand and went then, and ever since I have been sitting on my bed, trying to get things finally sorted out. This is really the first breather we have had since we turned our backs on the Victoria Bank.

I remember how bewildered the manager looked the day we broke it to him.

"*Both* of you?" he said. "You mean to tell me you *both* want to fly off and be nurses? But why? Tell me that."

We looked at one another, and I tried to explain. "One of those things, Mr. Hyde. Like—like ink in the veins or wanting to go on the stage. It hits you suddenly. You know."

He turned his big ebony ruler over and over in his thick white fingers and pushed out his bottom lip in a way that meant he was being obstinate. It was the way he looked at overdraft-hunters. "No. I don't know." There was a heavy silence in his mahogany-paneled office.

Peta broke in impatiently. "Didn't you feel the same at our age? Didn't you ever have the urge to be a—an engine driver, or a racing driver, or a football player? Or even a bank manager?"

"Never," Mr. Hyde said firmly. "Never." He took off his glasses and polished them irritably on the maroon handkerchief from his breast pocket. Then he rammed them back on his nose again and tucked in his chin to look over the top of them. "All I ever wanted to be, Miss Royde, was a ship's engineer." A faint pink flush appeared on his padded cheekbones. "Since you inquire."

"Then why—"

He blinked at us. "Why? I don't know why. It just worked out this way. Things do, you know. Not many people can choose their work, let me tell you. You're very fortunate to have parents who allow it. Very fortunate."

I have a sneaking feeling that he was a little jealous. And he ought to have remembered that Peta hasn't any parents to consult—she just borrows father and calls him "Uncle Bob."

Then he went on, "I suppose you've thought about the financial angle? That you'll be the poorer by about two hundred a year?"

It was the last thing we'd considered, but Peta wasn't going to admit it. "Yes, Mr. Hyde," she agreed smoothly. "Just at first. Then you'll accept a month's notice? We can leave at Christmas?"

"I'd prefer the week after Christmas, if you can contain yourselves that long. You know perfectly well what that week is like for the cashiers—there's the balancing, and the New Year bonus for the Willingshaw's to get out and—"

"But that's quite all right," I assured him. "We've been offered vacancies for January 10, Mr. Hyde. We can make it."

We made it. Our uniforms were delivered only two days before we were due here at St. Timothy's, with all the name marking to do on fourteen aprons, three dresses and umpteen cuffs, collars and caps apiece, but we made it. In fact, we landed here five hours before Braich-Jones, who unaccountably boarded the wrong train in Welshpool, and finished in Crewe instead of Birmingham—rather like the heroine of *Oh, Mr. Porter,* as Peta remarked—a mistake that we now know was quite foreign to her nature. She blames it on an altered railway timetable, but Peta, who reads psychology for fun, calls it "subconscious motivation." I can't imagine anyone having secret desires to visit Crewe so that sounds a bit farfetched. On the other hand, Braich-Jones's most irritating characteristic is that she simply doesn't make mistakes.

But all that was six weeks ago. Tonight, of all nights,

I suppose I ought to have gone to bed early as the other two have done; but I don't want today to end yet. Besides, I have not quite finished adjusting myself.

There is so much to adjust to. Even names. It has taken me all of six weeks in the preliminary training school to get used to the idea that from now on Peta will be plain Royde. It is a little easier to remember that I must never address Braich-Jones as Eirlys: for one thing she has already had some training and arrived here sophisticated enough to get off on the right foot from the beginning; for another, I am most unlikely to be tempted, because I haven't a clue how to pronounce it, though I would hazard a guess it has a dying fall, like her lilting mid-Wales voice.

It seems that here in hospital Christian names are used only accidently by ex-Lambs newly emerged from the P.T.S. and deliberately by the mature and privileged three-stripe seniors. It is not at all easy to think of myself as Elliot: I have to remind myself constantly that I shed my Lucy skin when I first snaked into this long, blue polka-dot dress that is to be my protective coloring for the next two years, until I exchange it for the check gingham of a third-year student.

Tonight—or so Braich-Jones remarked at teatime—we three are nothing more than starched shadows, because at midday a frightened little flock of new Lambs ousted us from the schoolroom, and we shall not have the full franchise of the wards until tomorrow. We have ceased to be Lambs, but we have not yet become nurses.

Tomorrow, dozens of confident, striding people whose names we have never heard will call us "nurse," and while this is in some ways an exhilarating prospect, Peta and I know perfectly well that we shall blush madly every time anyone actually does, however hardened Braich-Jones may be.

We have not yet been told to which wards we are to

report. This, the ultimate revelation, will be denied us until 6:50 A.M. tomorrow, when night sister will read out our names after breakfast. Peta—or rather, Royde—considers this an excellent arrangement. She declares that if she knew definitely, for example, that she was down for Ward 2, she would certainly decamp this evening. On the other hand, if she knew she was destined for the children's ward she would not be able to sleep for relief and excitement, and would then be too tired to make a good impression on Sister Hawthorn who, according to Braich-Jones's elder sister, is nothing but a pink-faced child herself.

We were discussing our prospects at teatime. Braich-Jones ticked off the wards on her thin brown fingers and gave us the benefit of her sister's knowledge. "Ward 1," she began. "Sister Peatman. Bright, but not beautiful—and not known to be patient with new probationers. Then on Ward 2—let's not dwell on that—there's this revolting ex-army type, Heywood-Bence."

"She's been at St. Tim's for donkey's years, hasn't she?" Royde interrupted. "Sister Tutor says so."

"Since the year dot. My dear, she's Timothy's trained—she must have arrived with the foundations, I should think."

"Three's not bad," I mused. "Sister Tetley looks rather sweet. Motherly. And on Ward 4 there's only a staff nurse, I know, because they're advertising for a new ward sister. Who's on Ward 5?"

Braich-Jones narrowed her dark eyes. "Let's think—oh, Sister Guthrie, broad Scots and the devil of a temper Greta says. Six is rather a duck, but I can't think of her name. On the top floor there's a niminy-priminy person called Harrowby and a fair jolly one who limps."

We could have gone on all day working our way through the operating rooms, and Outpatients and the other departments, only we hadn't time. We had to give up our seats to the next batch of people hurrying in for tea.

One of them, a gentle creature with great brown eyes, nodded at us and said, "Make the most of it, chicks. Tomorrow you'll have to suffer like the rest of us."

I grinned. "Where are you?"

"Six." She sank into a chair and reached wearily for the butter dish. "Sister Pegg's all right. But we're not due for a new probationer; we had one last time they let the Lambs out. One of you might go to Ward 8—I know they're shorthanded. That's Sister Fisher, and she's a tartar. You mustn't let that limp-eyed baby face mislead you!" She glanced up the table. "You'd better hop it. Home sister's nattering to Cook, and she's looking scalpels."

"That's Sylvia Noble." Braich-Jones informed us on the stairs. "Used to be a ballet dancer, Greta says. She must be cracked to drop that for this. She didn't begin to train until she was twenty-five, Greta says."

"Greta says" is rapidly becoming a catchword. Still, if it were not for some of the things Greta Braich-Jones has said at one time or another, we might be feeling even more at sea than we do already. She's a staff nurse in Outpatients, and she ought to know, and at least we have some clue what to expect when we go on the wards. If we had only heard Sister Tutor's version, which seems to be largely geared down to the prehistory of the days before registration, we might be all set to make idiots of ourselves. Tut is very decent, but she doesn't move with the times. We shall probably drop plenty of bricks, as it is. . . .

Home sister has just been in to tell me that it is tenthirty and time my light was out. She goggled at me when she flung the door open, and said, "Not even undressed yet, Nurse Elliot?" and scowled. And then she added, "You go on the wards tomorrow, don't you? Well, I suppose it's quite an occasion. Very well, nurse. Have your light out in ten minutes, there's a good girl."

So—since she is almost certain to come back and check my light, because, Greta says, she is that kind—this is almost the end of the beginning. But it will take more than home sister to bully me out of keeping a diary. I promised father I would, and it is the first promise he has ever asked me to make in my life. One promise in nearly twenty years is not so much to ask.

I suppose that because mother was a nurse when he first met her he is reliving it, as it were, through me, now that he is alone. I just hope I make it. I hope I can be as good a nurse as they say she was, bless her, though it seems a pretty soaring ambition right now. Mother was a gold medalist at Bart's—and though Tim's is definitely well thought of, it isn't in the same class. And I doubt whether I am in mother's class, either. She must have been really something for anyone as choosy as father to have gone on thinking about her all these years.

February 22

AT LAST we know the worst. Braich-Jones is on Ward 2, with the paralyzing Sister Heywood-Bence—more usually known, we gather, as "the gorgon." Royde is on Ward 7, which is a men's surgical ward and something of an ordeal, but she says Sister Harrowby will not be on duty until tomorrow, so that the full horror has not yet burst upon her.

And I am the lucky one, after all. Not that I dare to be too cock-a-hoop about landing in the children's ward because Sister Hawthorn says it is only a temporary arrangement, while her other junior, Prescott, is off duty with an inflamed toe. Of course, Braich-Jones, who has had training, is better fitted to withstand the rigors of Ward 2 than I am, but it never seemed to me that I should come in for the children.

The staff nurse from our ward, a tall, fair, angelic-looking creature named Anna Dodman, collared me outside the dining room and said, ''After chapel, nurse, you just hang onto me, will you?''

When I said, ''Right-ho,'' she smiled and walked on ahead, but Braich-Jones dug her bony elbow into my ribs and coughed.

''You don't say 'right-ho' to a staff nurse,'' she hissed. ''You say, 'Yes, staff,' and don't keep on walking when she speaks to you. See?''

I nodded soberly. ''Yes, Nurse Braich-Jones!''

She let out her breath sharply. ''You don't care a bit, do you? If you'd been on the Isolation Ward with me you'd have had to toe the line.''

''You make it sound like a reformatory school.'' Royde was giggling. ''Dash it, we're not kids! You take all this protocol stuff too seriously. Why on earth should we—''

''Now, Nurse Royde,'' I said sharply. ''Hurry along to chapel, please! You know night sister doesn't like to be kept waiting. Remember what Tut taught us—'hospital etiquette is common politeness officially expressed.' The uniform, not the woman, my sweet.''

We filed into chapel and waited while night sister persuaded one of the seniors to play the organ for the hymn. I didn't know the tune, and there were no hymnbooks in the back row, so I just went on thinking how lucky I was to be going to Sister Hawthorn and how beautiful Staff Dodman was.

Four of us fell in with staff outside chapel. There was a plump dark third-year student named Jevons and a couple of ''dotty frocks'' who introduced themselves as Bradford and Parry. And then a nurse in navy blue, wearing a flowing army cap, joined us and said, ''I wonder whether my patient's still with us?''

"If I know anything about Garry Wilson," Bradford said, "we shall be a night nurse short, not a patient!"

Staff turned to me. "Garry is a very spoiled little boy. He's been very ill with pneumonia and Private Nurse Dale had had her hands full. It's just as well his father insisted on paying for a special—we couldn't have coped without her. He's a live wire."

"I see, staff," I said intelligently. "I didn't know people paid for specials. I thought the doctors simply ordered them when they were necessary."

She smiled, and I noticed how blue her eyes were. "They do, of course, when a case merits it. But even if it doesn't, the relatives can still have one by paying. And sometimes they send the kids' own nannies in."

"But—" I frowned, and tried to remember what Braich-Jones had said about specialing, apart from commenting that it was a plummy job. "If all the hospitals are understaffed, how can nurses ever be spared to special?"

"A good question. They can't, sometimes. But we can get private nurses in, like nurse Dale. Mind, it's been better in a lot of places since they allowed part-timers and married nurses living out. But matron isn't keen. All Tim's nurses are either in training or on the permanent staff." She looked me over. "You didn't come straight from school. What have you been doing? Any training?"

I explained about the bank and how I'd more or less followed Royde there from Beechington High, the way she had now been infected with my nursing fever. "But mother was a nurse," I mentioned.

"Then don't tell a soul. If you do, you'll be expected to know a lot more than you do. And if Braich-Jones had any gumption she'd keep quiet about it and appear to shine." She waited while I opened the ward door for her—at least I knew that much.

"I'll warn her," I promised. "But it's probably too late. She's rather keen on telling us that if we'd been there we wouldn't have lasted a week and all that."

Nurse Jevons called me into the ward kitchen and showed me where to keep my cuffs in a drawer marked "Day nurses." "Any personal possessions you bring on the ward," she told me, "go in there. Except your cape—you hang that outside the clinical room."

I said I hadn't thought to bring it up, which wasn't strictly true. It had seemed to me that nobody in her senses would be seen dead walking about in a blue serge cape lined with red flannel. I'd assumed it was just a kind of ceremonial dress that was part of the tradition.

"Then you should. It can be mighty cold, traipsing about these corridors down to the dispensary and the departments; and if you don't wear it somebody will tear you off a strip sooner or later. Now you'd better go and help Parry with the beds."

I pushed open the swing doors and followed the other first-year student. I had always thought of the wards as being quiet, hushed places. That just shows how wrong you can be. There was an earsplitting din going on in the main ward. Most of the thirty children were standing up in their cots bawling, "Good morning, dear nurses, good morning to you." They looked like a pack of elves in their scarlet bed jackets. And even the babies in the cubicles beyond the long glass wall were all waving their arms and legs.

When the bigger ones spotted me a squeal of, "New nurse! New nurse!" went down the long ward, from one bed to the next. It was highly embarrassing. I tried to imagine what it would have been like if I'd stayed with Mr. Hyde long enough to get my own till and all the customers had bellowed "New cashier" at the sight of me. I think Mr. Hyde would take a dim view, but it didn't seem to bother staff. She only laughed and flapped her hand at them as she passed with the thermometer tray.

"Take no notice," Parry said. "They'll calm down. They're always like this for the first ten minutes, but they soon get tired of it."

We began at the far end of the ward, making the beds, throwing the blankets over a chair. "I'll hold them, you pull the drawsheet through," Parry told me.

"Aren't we supposed to turn the mattresses?" I lugged the first sheet through and tucked it in concertinawise, as Tut had taught us. "Or do we do that at night?"

She looked at me as if I were mad. "These are rubber mattresses. You don't have to turn them." Something else Tut hadn't told us.

We worked our way along, pulling, tucking, mitering the corners of the red blankets the children's ward used for bedspreads. At nearly every cot, I had my cap pulled off. One curly-headed toddler retreated to her pillow methodically crushing my carefully set gathers to a pulp. "If you don't mind, ducky," I said. "That happens to be my best Sunday hat."

"I'm not Ducky," she told me solemnly. "I'm Jacqueline. And I always squeeze the nurses' caps."

"Not mine, you don't. Unless you want to quarrel with me. Do you?"

She shook her head. "No. You're a nice lady."

"Thanks so much. Then perhaps I can have it back. If night sister sees me without it she'll have me shot. You've no idea!"

She screeched with laughter as Parry swung her out of her cot. Parry sighed. "Come on, Elliot, do. We shall never get done at this rate. Never mind your cap—you'll have to change it at first lunch."

I jerked the sheet through. "Now I know why we

need so many. I thought it was a mistake when they were delivered. Imagine that!''

"You'll think a lot more things are mistakes before you've finished. And if we don't have these beds done before sister gets here, that'll be a mistake, too."

She showed me how to turn the cot casters inward, so that people wouldn't trip over them and reminded me that all the pillows much have their open ends away from the ward door.

"But why?"

She shrugged. "Don't expect a reason for everything because half the time there isn't one. Tidiness, I suppose—one of the Crimean hangovers. It has to be so, that's all. Same as turning all the sheets down fourteen inches."

I snorted. "How can you tell when it's fourteen inches? You don't measure them. Or do you?"

"For heaven's sake, Elliot! You just get to know, I suppose. By experience." She stood at the door and peered down the ward, looking for trouble, with her sandy eyebrows close together. Then she glanced up at the big clock on the wall, its red second hand ticking away the precious moments. "Sister will be here at eight o'clock," she told me. "You've got just five minutes to collect all those comics off the windowsills and wash all the locker tops."

"Right. Where do I find the things?"

"Where do you think? In the splint cupboard? In the sluice room, of course. Out through the middle door, and turn left. Right's the bathroom, and the mattress room and toy room are in the middle. Now have you got it? Because I want to get the drinks ready."

I plunged down the ward again, slithering on the shiny floor that the ward maid, Ruby, was desultorily polishing with her heavy bumper. The bright eyes in the cots watched every move, and Jacqueline made an abortive dive at me as I passed her. Tut had shown us around one of the wards, but it was in the other wing and not arranged quite like this one. I dreaded the moment when somebody would ask me to find something—Braich-Jones says every nurse's secret dread is that some doctor will ask her to find or do something she has never heard of. I had no idea where anything was kept, except linen, which we are not allowed to take without asking. But I managed to find a bowl and a cotton rag, and I sketchily washed the marble locker tops with one eye on the clock.

It wasn't easy because some of them had candy stuck to them, and others had been scribbled on, and I still had two left to do when Sister Hawthorn came on duty. She sat down at her table just inside the ward door, with the senior night nurse standing behind her, putting her cuffs on, and the junior in the background still ticking off her bath list.

Before she began to read the night report from the enormous book in front of her, sister looked quickly down the ward and waved to the children. Then she leaned back to look up at Nurse Hodgetts, the senior. "We've a new probationer, then, nurse?"

"Yes, sister. Nurse Elliot."

"Good. Now—how is the family? Everybody all right?" She bent her frilly cap over the report and read steadily down the long page, while I washed away at the sticky marble of Jacqueline's locker.

I had put the bowl away and was trying vaguely to tidy the sluice room when she began her round. She came out to me and said, "Good morning, Nurse Elliot. I hope you are finding you way around?"

I didn't say right-ho this time. I remembered to stand up straight and say, "Yes, sister. Thank you, sister." Tut would have been very pleased with me, I felt, after the hours she had put in teaching us to say just that and to keep our arms behind our backs when we had no cuffs on. (Peta had remarked at the time that Tut must have trained in the days when people put pantalets on piano legs—it seemed to fill her with horror to think that anyone, especially housemen, should catch a glimpse of our bare flesh, or even know that nurses really had forearms and not just sleeves with hands at the end of them.)

She smiled at me, and I thought how pretty she was, with her heart-shaped face and big blue gray eyes, although she was not really young. And then I asked, "What ought I to do with all this dirty bed linen, sister? Send it to the laundry?"

Her mouth twitched. "I'm afraid not. Not until you've sluiced it, nurse. That is one of the unpleasant jobs the junior has to do—so you must make the best of it." She showed me how to use the sluice brush on the drawsheets and baby squares and where to hang them to dry on the balcony railings. "Don't put anything in the laundry basket until it's almost dry, will you, nurse?" Her eyes twinkled. "Or we shall have the laundress up here to reprimand us!"

"I won't, sister," I promised.

"You and Nurse Parry are responsible for this room's tidiness at all times. Nurse Bradford looks after the bathroom and mattress room, and we all try to help to keep the toy room tidy. Do your best to keep it straight—it's all much easier if you clear up as you go."

"Yes, sister. Thank you, sister."

She went out again then and left me to it, and I was hard at it until Parry came in and said, "You're to go to first break. Hop it, or you'll be late—it's after nine. Half an hour, remember."

I grabbed my cuffs from the kitchen drawer and was halfway along the flat before I remembered something else Tut had dinned into us. We didn't do anything or go anywhere without permission. And I hadn't reported to sister. I turned back to where she was charting temperatures in the baby section. "May I go, please, sister?"

"Yes, nurse. And bring the drums back with you will you? They should be ready by now."

I had no idea what she meant, but I said, "Yes, sister," once more. Then I walked across the garden to the home, wishing that I'd had the sense to carry my cape. There was a hoar frost all over the rustic work and on the withered chrysanthemum plants in the borders, and I was shivering by the time I reached the porch.

I made my bed and changed my apron, and tried to hurry a fresh cap into shape. It looked like a pudding, but there was not time to be finicky if I was to call in for a cup of coffee in the dining room. As it was, I had to drink it standing up or leave half of it and go without my hunk of bread and cheese because I was afraid I wouldn't be back on the ward by nine-thirty.

And it was only after I had chased up the stairs to our flat that I remembered what sister had said about bringing the drums back. I stood on one leg trying to make sense of it. Drums? Dressing drums, presumably. But where did I fetch them from? There were three sterilizing rooms, I knew that much; one near Outpatients, one in the theater block and one behind the mortuary. Which could it be? This was something Tut had *not* told us, so far as I could remember. Nor had Greta uttered any words of wisdom along those lines that would help.

I tried the nearest one first, in the theater block, across the iron bridge of the surgical wing. All the Lambs are taken to see the theaters, so I knew just where to look. As I'd hoped, there were stacks of drums outside the door.

The trouble was, I had no idea which were ours. Most of them were numbered, but as far as I know the children's ward doeesn't have a number. There seemed to be nobody about to ask, so I went ferreting my way through the pile. And at last I found two big square drums with tags marked "C" on their handles.

When I'd dragged them from the bottom of the stack I realized they were extremely heavy, but I dangled one from each hand and set off across the bridge again. Halfway across I dropped one of them, with a clatter like twenty garbage cans. Unfortunately it didn't simply fall on the bridge—it also managed to turn over and slide out into space under the handrail.

Just in time, I saw the glimmer of a white coat underneath on the ground floor, two stories below. I yelled like a cowboy. Two arms came up as the drum plummeted down, and whoever he was sat flat on the path, with the drum in his lap.

I leaned over the rail, trembling with relief. "I'm terribly sorry. I dropped it."

"That's known as stating the obvious," he called up. "You've probably crippled me for life. You'd better come down and fetch the damn thing—I'm incapable of climbing up there with it!"

I raced down the stairs and out onto the path. He was sitting on the drum lighting a cigarette, and he looked up and said, "Well? So it was you, was it? Wretched girl!"

He had a blunt, happy sort of face and rough brown hair, and he looked as though he might be somebody's brother. Also he was laughing, which was a relief. When I'd apologized again he asked, "Where were you taking the thing, anyway?"

"Children's ward," I explained. "There are two of them, and they're mighty heavy. That's why—"

He sighed and got up. "You win. Go on—you get the other, and I'll bring this one for you. Mr. Big Heart, that's me."

I looked at his white jacket and wondered who he was, but there was no way of telling without asking him. So I retrieved the other drum and let him follow me to the ward. When he had dumped his load in the lobby outside the swing doors he saluted and hurried away again, and that was that.

Staff frowned and said, "Where on earth have you been, nurse? Did you get lost? You were due back ages ago."

It sounded pretty thin, but said I'd been to get the drums and hadn't been able to find them straight away.

"Very well. You're off duty from ten till half-past twelve today. Will you just collect the mugs, and straighten the castors again before you go? And when you go down, take the dispensary basket with you, too."

"Yes, staff. What do I do with it?"

"All the empties are in it with the book. Leave it outside the dispensary near the hatch. You know the way?" I nodded. "And when you come back before lunch collect it again. Clear?"

It is twelve o'clock now, and I shall soon have to go. We don't get any extra time for going down to the dispensary, and it's quite a walk through Outpatients corridor and down a tunnel affair. I must remember to ask Braich-Jones, when I see her, whether the men in white have any distinguishing marks. They can't all be doctors, because there are lab people, and theater technicians and porters, too, all looking alike. There must be some way of telling which is which and knowing whether or not they are important. That is just one more thing Tut forgot to explain to us in the P.T.S.—with malice aforethought, I daresay. But I expect Greta Braich-Jones has a formula.

February 23

I SIMPLY HADN'T the heart to write any more last night. For one thing, my feet were aching so much by half-past eight that I only wanted to die quietly in a corner, without fuss. I compromised by lying on my bed with my bare feet up on the top rail, and it is difficult to write legibly in that position—besides, there are the direst penalties for getting ink on our bedspreads because the home is still new enough to be a bit of a showpiece. But worse than just being exhausted, I have already done the "wrong thing," as Sister Hawthorn adequately pointed out to me.

When I'd collected the dispensary basket and managed to get back to the ward by half-past twelve yesterday, Parry met me by the kitchen door. "You're for it," she said. "Sister wants you the second you come on duty. How can you be so clueless?" She vanished into the kitchen, and I dumped the basket in the clinical room and went to find sister. I remembered to keep my cuffs on.

She was behind screens at the end of the ward doing a dressing. "Take your cuffs off, nurse, and hold this child's leg," she said quietly. "Put your hands under the sterile towel, please. Thank you."

I put my hands firmly on the little boy's leg, so that he shouldn't wriggle, and knelt there beside the cot watching her swabbing, probing and cleaning, until I felt quite faint. She glanced at me quickly and said, "Ronny has osteomyelitis, nurse. It's been very long and tedious for him—and painful. But he's a good boy."

That was a rebuke. In other words, if Ronny could take it, I could. I took a deep breath and said, "Yes, sister."

When she had laid gauze and wool on the long, ugly wound, she told me to put on a figure-eight bandage, and I managed it all right, except that it went on from without inward instead of the proper way, but she didn't say anything. When I had put the flowered screens away at the end of the ward, she called me into the linen room and asked for my teaching chart, and gave me a tick for "assisting with surgical dressings." Then she said, "Nurse, when I told you to bring back the drums, why didn't you?"

"But I did, sister! Two. Big ones. I left them in the lobby."

"And didn't your own common sense tell you that you wouldn't be expected to carry things that size? Didn't it occur to you that those were not ward drums at all?"

I blinked. "No sister. They were heavy, but I thought—"

"To begin with, nurse, I'm perfectly certain Sister Tutor must have shown you where the ward drums are sterilized. The autoclave near Outpatients is the one we use. The theater sterilizing room is quite sacred. Didn't you know that?"

"No, sister."

"Well, you know now, I hope. But that isn't all. Why did you bring those particular drums out of all there must have been to choose from?"

"They—they were marked 'C,' sister. I thought it stood for children's. I thought I *was* using my common sense, sister. I'm sorry."

"They are *not* marked 'C,' nurse. That was wishful thinking. They were marked 'G'—for gloves." She sighed. "What you did, nurse, was to run off with the theater's entire supply of sterile gloves. They had no idea where they were, and staff hadn't noticed them here, so it was a long time before they ran them to earth."

I bit my lip. "Really, sister, I'm awfully sorry. I had no idea—"

"With the result, nurse," she plowed dutifully on, "that Dr. Welby—who is our senior consultant surgeon and not a person to be trifled with—was kept waiting half an hour to begin his list. Now you see what you did?"

If I hadn't noticed the flicker in her eyes, I think I might have descended to salt tears. As it was, I felt about an inch high. It was like the time Mr. Hyde sent for me because I had a customer a hundred pounds in the red through pushing the wrong button on one of the bank's horrid little green machines. "It might have been a matter of life and death," was what he said. I wondered why Sister Hawthorn, who was entitled to say it, didn't.

She just said, "That will be all, nurse. Now get on with your routine as quickly as you can. There are the children's dinner crocks to collect and the whole ward to bedpan. And then they must all settle down for half an hour while the ward is tidied ready for visitors." And since then she hasn't said another word about it.

In the evening I asked Braich-Jones about all these white coats. "Such a rash of them," I complained. "I don't see how you know whether you're being impertinent to a top surgeon or obsequious to a porter. It's most confusing."

She put on a superior expression. "Greta says," she began (I might have known Greta would have a word for it), "Greta says they're all quite different if you look closely. Their shoes for instance. You can't mistake a lab boy for a consultant, even if they both wear white coats. Listen—seniors, long; juniors, short. And doctors have breast pockets, technicians don't. Besides, you don't see consultants trotting about on their own. They always have their housemen with them. See?"

"Thanks," I said. "Clear as mud. Doesn't get me anywhere. What I'm trying to do is to identify the body—a young man I nearly liquidated."

"Well, it's simple enough. What was he wearing?"

"Short jacket and scruffy shoes. What does that make him?"

"Pockets?"

"I just can't remember. He had a nice voice if that helps."

"It doesn't," she said. "They all have. What's known as 'received standard English,' I believe. But why do you want to know who he is?"

I stared at her. "Why, because— Yes, you're right. Why, indeed?"

I saw him again this morning. Sister doled out clean top sheets for all the cots and remarked that it was Dr. Clifford's round day. He appears to be the pediatrician who looks after most of the medical children. Most of the surgical ones seem to be under Dr. Dinsmore-Todd.

When the ward was spanking tidy, all the castors turned in and all the pillows facing the proper way, sister showed me what we had to put out on the center table for rounds—the patella hammer, the opthalmoscope, the sphygmomanometer and a jar of wooden spatulas for looking at throats with a flashlight. "If I signal to you, nurse, as I go round with Dr. Clifford, it will be because I want something from here. The house physician carries all the forms in his pocket so you needn't worry about those."

"I see, sister."

"And nurse—remember to put on your cuffs as soon as Dr. Clifford arrives."

I said I would, though I couldn't really see the point. And when sister zoomed over to the door, smoothing her apron and tweaking her strings into place under her chin, I rolled my sleeves down and joined the procession.

Dr. Clifford is a tall, very thin man, with a haggard face, and he doesn't talk at all. His hair is just beginning to go gray over his ears, and he is the personification of secret sorrow. Oddly enough, the children seem to like him very much—and I didn't realize why until I watched him examining one of them. He is extraordinarily gentle. He had long bony fingers with spatulate tips, and they seem to be listening instead of feeling, when he touches a patient.

But the interesting thing is that his H.P. turns out to be the young man I almost concussed. His name, Nurse Parry says, is William Blunt, which is a perfect name for him. Unfortunately it is wasted on him because it seems that everyone who knows him calls him Buster—which is one consolation for not knowing him well. Buster isn't a name I'd wish on a mongrel terrier.

I called father this evening and told him as much as I could remember of what I've been doing. He said that Mr. Hyde had been asking after me and was there any news of Peta.

"No," I confessed. "I really ought to have gone along to her room this evening, but to be truthful I haven't seen her today at all. All I know is that she's on a male surgical ward, and as far as I'm aware she's still alive and kicking. Anyhow, whatever you do, don't let Mr. Hyde think we have any regrets. I'd hate him to say 'I told you so.'"

Father laughed. "As a matter of fact, he thought you both had plenty of guts to make a fresh start. He was very complimentary."

"That's fine coming now," I grumbled. "He didn't say that at the time—he was taking the line that the hospital's loss was his gain as it were. So he misses us, does he?"

"He does. He was telling me how difficult it is to get intelligent girls to stay in banks. He still has only one—he can't find another."

I said he could have Royde back, if he liked, but that he had had me. "But how are *you*?" I asked him.

"Fine. Managed to get a game of golf yesterday, with Major Martin. That's where I saw Hyde."

"Father! He doesn't play golf? He isn't human enough."

"He does. He's a four-handicap man as a matter of fact. Amazing, isn't it?"

I was silent. The idea of Mr. Hyde gallivanting on the golf course was more than I could accept. I could imagine his using his ebony ruler instead of a putter.

Father said, "By the way, you forgot your clubs. Shall I send them? You'll be getting a game sometime, I suppose?"

"You can suppose away," I retorted. "I have legs. On the end of them are two feet. Don't I know it! Do you really think golf is quite the game a nurse wants to play? I think I'll take up chess. That is, if I ever have time to take up anything at all."

He laughed. "I'll send them down anyhow or find time to bring them. I told you I'd be in Liverpool for a week or two, didn't I? I shall go on Friday, I expect. I'll let you know where I'll be staying."

"Is it a big job?"

"Fairly. Hospital extensions. They liked my design for the isolation ward at Leicester, apparently."

"A pity you can't come and design some extensions here," I told him. "A Turkish bath for tired staff for example."

Before I settled down I went along to Royde's room, but she wasn't there. I met Braich-Jones as I came out and she said, "Haven't you heard? Casualty number one. She's off sick."

"Oh, what's wrong?"

Braich-Jones winked. "Acute Harrowbyitis, I

wouldn't wonder. And who shall blame her for that? How's children's?"

"Fine. How's Ward 2? Or don't we talk about that?"

"I can take it. I've met 'em. But if she throws that temperature book at me just once more—"

"I've found out who he is," I remarked irrelevantly. "He's D. Clifford's H.P., and they call him Buster of all things."

She smiled pityingly. "Now isn't that nice? But remember, you're not supposed to fraternize with the housemen. It distracts from the career, and matron doesn't like it. So you be careful."

I can't imagine why Braich-Jones thought it necessary to say all that. I put it on record that I am no more interested in Dr. Clifford's H.P. than I am in Dr. Clifford himself.

CHAPTER TWO

February 27

THE LAST THREE DAYS have been a mad rush, and when I look back the outstanding impression is one of aching feet. At least, a great many more things did happen, but I can only concentrate on them in a horizontal position, which is hopeless for writing them down. Braich-Jones says nurses ought to be properly shod, like horses, but I feel this would do very little for the ward floors, and I can't imagine what Ruby would say.

What Ruby will say seems to matter a great deal. Last night I spilled about a teaspoonful of water in front of sister's table, and she looked at me with fear in her eyes and said, "Oh, nurse! Polish it quickly, before Ruby sees it!" It hardly seems a rational attitude, but (Greta says) this is a universal evil—a sister has to go on living with the same ward maid while nurses come and go, and if she doesn't keep her sweet and sunny her life isn't worth living. And things spilled on floors are a ward maid's pet hate, I gather. But at least I don't think Sister Hawthorn uses Ruby as an informer, which is one of the things that "the gorgon" does to perfection. Braich-Jones says that on Ward 2 they have a lot of trouble hiding their peccadilloes from Agnes, who is as all-seeing as the Lord's Day Observance Society and has a regular tell session with Sister Heywood-Bence every morning while she has her elevenses.

Our trio has been reduced to a couple—Peta seems to

have caught diphtheria from somewhere, and home sister has been having an immunization campaign and doing things to our rooms that make them smell like an oil-and-colorman's shop. It is rather ironic that she has been shipped off to the isolation hospital Braich-Jones came from, so I have written to her to find out whether there is anything known, as the police put it. Not that I dislike Braich-Jones—but I would dearly love to take the wind from her sails when occasion arises because she is always so depressingly right. If only she had once done something foolish, it would be a great comfort to me.

They let me see Peta before she was wafted away—home sister made me put on a gown and mask and gargle afterward—and she was very depressed. She said, "You know, Lucy, I don't think I can do it. Nursing, I mean."

"But why? You were all for it. You were, weren't you?"

She nodded and swallowed painfully. "But it was all theory. Real people are quite different. I mean—they're perfect strangers, and—" Then she burst into tears—a thing I've never known her to do—and wailed, "I wish I were back in the bank with the beastly machines. I don't mind handling them."

"Shucks!" I said. "You're tired, that's all. You can't handle people by remote control." I left her to it then because I simply didn't understand why she felt that way. Home sister stopped me in the corridor and actually smiled at me.

"Nurse Royde seems very depressed," she said. "You don't think she's homesick, do you, nurse?"

I said she hadn't anything to be homesick for, except maybe the bank. "I think it's the men," I told her. "I think perhaps it scared her, going to a male ward. She might be better with children."

Home sister raised her eyebrows. "Indeed, Nurse Elliot? That's what you'd prescribe, is it?"

My face went hot, and I looked down at my feet. "I mean—the children are so nice, it might cheer her up, sister."

"You may be right," she nodded. "But that's for matron to say, isn't it?" She rustled away down the corridor, and I could have kicked myself.

I was not the least surprised when Sister Hawthorn called me after lunch. "I told you this was only temporary, didn't I, nurse? I'm afraid you'll be moving again tomorrow—Nurse Prescott will be back on duty."

"You don't know where I'll be going, do you, sister?"

"No, nurse. I'm afraid I don't. But it isn't of very much importance, is it? Before you've finished your training you'll have worked in all the wards and departments, I expect. You must do your best in each one, as it comes along."

I said, "Yes, sister; thank you, sister," and went out and got on with the sluice room, which Parry had left up to its eyes for me. In addition to my own bucket of sluicing, she had left her own, as well, instead of doing it before she went off duty. It was no use leaving it there—sister would say it was up to me to keep the place tidy. But if I had left mine it would have been different, I daresay. That is the penalty of being the junior probationer on a ward—whatever anyone else leaves undone always seems to be the junior's job, whether it's the other junior's linen bucket or bandages the seniors have forgotten to wash or even a fire that Ruby hasn't bothered to make up. If father could see my hands he would never believe them; they look as red and chapped as though I had been scrubbing steps all week in the frost.

I wish I knew where I was going tomorrow. If I go to Ward 7 to replace Royde it will not be so bad—but I may not. But a women's ward doesn't appeal in the least. It is much harder work (Greta says, of course) because women are much more demanding than men. They are also rather good at putting the poison down with sister, which men would scorn to do.

I have a note from father giving me his Liverpool hotel number, but I shall wait to phone until I know where I am going.

February 28

WE HAVE longer passes on Sundays, and I am technically off from 5:30 until 10:00 P.M., but it was after six o'clock when I finally got off the ward, so by the time I'd changed it was too late to go to church.

Ward 7 is not bad after all. I was quite resigned to it by the time night sister read out my name after breakfast. In any case, it is Sister Harrowby's long weekend, so we have not yet met, and Staff Haarstein—who is a Norwegian doing an exchange—doesn't speak English well enough to be peremptory in it. She uses such expressions as, "Please to distribute to the patients their drinks, nurse, if you please." All very slowly and precisely in a high, flat voice, with her pale blue eyes very anxious. And when I broke a thermometer and went to tell her, she just said, "This is not good, no? Six pennies from you I must collect, if you please. This is not good. I am angry." I don't think she was—she shows no emotion at all. She is really very good-looking, in a Burne-Jonesey sort of a way, but utterly lacking in life, which is a pity. If she showed a little more animation, the men would adore her—as it is she scares them into dumbness.

The men were a surprise. When we arrived in the ward this morning, I was nervous. I thought I would have to run the gauntlet of their looks in silence. But they are quite as noisy as the children, if not more so, and have exactly the same habit of singing, "Good morning, dear nurses, good morning to you." What's more, they also called out "New nurse!" and told one another to look at me. I nearly dived back into the kitchen out of stage fright, but staff followed me into the ward and reduced it all to cool fact by saying, "This is a new nurse, yes. She is Nurse Ell-i-ot. You will not shout at her, please," in her quiet monotone, and they stopped yelling and contented themselves with grinning as I passed them.

Sylvia Noble has moved up here, too, and she is a much nicer person to work with than Parry was. We did the beds together to begin with, and she told me all the men's names and what was wrong with them as we went. Most of them are fairly young, but there are a few older ones, mostly in the three side wards, which are quieter for them, and the juniors don't look after those.

The last bed we came to was empty. "I expect Mr. Collins is out in the kitchen," Noble said as she flung back the top blanket onto the chair I'd put at the foot of the bed. "At least, I hope he is."

I stripped off the next blanket and the sheet and jerked out the rubber draw sheet. "You hope he is? Why?"

Noble opened her big dark eyes at me. "Because if he isn't we shall have to do the drinks ourselves. And I'm not used to it—they spoil us here."

I stared. "You mean—the patients are allowed to help?"

"Not allowed, no. Not when sister's on duty. But they love to help—and I think it's good for them. Bob Collins has done the drinks every morning this week—he's a dear. After all, when they get to the 'up' stage they get bored. They enjoy pottering about. That's the nice thing about male wards—no woman will ever do so much as roll a few swabs. They're here to make the most of being waited on, believe me."

"Oh, well," I said. "I suppose most housewives don't

get a rest unless they do come into hospital. You can't blame them." I folded the bedspread under the top, and mitered my corner. "Nobody seems to like female wards, though."

I took the bucket, and she took the back tray, and I followed her out into the annex.

"Women are fine when they're really ill," she said. "They're real stoics. But the moment they're convalescent, frankly, they behave like spoiled babies. Now when the men are really ill they make more fuss—they get windy, I think—but the first day they're allowed on their two feet for five minutes they want to help straight away. They'd do all the work for us if they were allowed to. They're so grateful and so glad they're better—they want to make some return. Because, of course, it's always the nurses who cured them, never the doctor. The women have no such illusions!"

"Women are realists," I suggested. "Men are sentimental." I began to count the laundry and realized for the first time that I had no sluicing to do, which was a joy. "I enjoyed the children," I added.

"Everyone does." Noble wiped the back bowl and put it on it's tray. "It's the nicest place to begin, I think. Breaks you in gently. I don't think your friend Nurse Royde enjoyed us much. I hear she's off with diph. Is she a particular friend of yours?"

"Sort of," I said. I leaned on the drain board to fill the laundry book. "But don't pull your punches just because of that. I want to know what upset her." I turned around. "What did?"

Noble's smile flickered in and out. "Sheer man fright, I think. She committed the unforgivable sin: she was embarrassed by the sight of thirty men in pajamas, I guess. It's fatal. Even if you are, you don't have to show it. Otherwise they'd curl up, you see."

"I know." I frowned. "But I'm not surprised." I explained that Peta was an orphan, that she'd led a pretty sheltered life and that she had even been shy of the men in the bank. "David Lathman used to ask her to go out with him regularly, every payday." I said. "But she'd been there a year before she ever did."

"And then?"

I groaned. "She walked out on him—left him sitting in a movie house, thinking she'd be back—because he held her hand."

Noble's face was a study, and then I remembered that she had probably mixed with plenty of men in her job as a ballet dancer. I wasn't going to admit to her that I was very nearly as inexperienced as Peta. It didn't seem to me that a few dances with father's friends at the golf-club dance really counted as experience.

"Too bad!" Noble said lightly. "Well—press on regardless. We'd better check on young Collins and get those drinks out. We don't do much spitting and polishing on Sundays, thank goodness. Just the locker tops."

Out in the ward a tall young man in a vermilion dressing gown was holding a feeding cup for a man with his leg up in an extension frame. He pushed his fair hair back and smiled at Noble. "Beaten you to it, nurse," he told her. "They're all given out. There's just Mr. Enderby to feed."

I remembered Mr. Enderby—he was at the far end of the ward in the half that was my responsibility. "I'll feed him," I said. "Is that his drink on the radiator?"

Bob Collins nodded. "Yes, I thought it'd keep hot on there. Have you come instead of Nurse Royde?" He looked me over, and I straightened my cap self-consciously. "Guess we frightened her!"

Noble laughed and took the cup from him. "It'll take more than you to frighten Nurse Elliot," she warned him. "She used to do a man's job let me tell you."

I escaped to Mr. Enderby. He was in a long plaster cast and couldn't sit up. "You must be sick of it," I told him. "How long do you have to be in it?" He looked too active a type to be stretched out in a hospital bed.

He rolled his eyes over the spout of the feeding cup. "Wish I knew. Slipped disc, they say. That's what rugger does for you."

"Oh? That's how you got it, is it?" He looked big and hefty. "Forward?"

"Front row. Somehow or other I managed to change places with the ball in a scrimmage. Had half the Old Silhillians sitting on me. Not nice."

"No," I agreed. "They're a tough lot."

His hazel eyes brightened. "You watch them, do you?"

"No. Not often. I'm a Old Veseyan follower myself. I've seen them at the O.V.'s ground, though; it was quite a match." I waited while he finished his drink and took the cup away and wiped his mouth. "Who do you play for?"

He grinned. "Not very observant are you? O.V.'s. Never noticed me on the field? With my red hair? There and I thought I was conspicuous!"

"Oh, but I haven't seen them this last two seasons," I explained. "You must have started playing since I stopped watching." I bent to put his locker cloth away in the cupboard. "Perhaps you've been away at university or something?"

"I was. I only came back to the team last year. Same time as Buster did."

I straightened up. "Buster? You mean Dr. Blunt— from the hospital?"

"That's right. You know him, I expect. Best halfback in the business. He—"

"Nurse Elliot," came Staff Haarstein's patient voice.

"I wish to tell you that you will go off duty at half-past five, please. That is understood?"

"Yes, staff." I began to collect the cups from the lockers. "What do I do next?"

"I wish to know, please, do you know how to help with dressings? You have done this?"

"Once," I admitted. "Only once."

"Then you will help me this morning. But first you must to go to the break, no?"

"Yes, staff," I agreed. "Now? Or later?"

"You go now. I shall be ready for your help when you return."

I spent most of the morning trotting around the beds with her pulling the dressing trolley along with us, boiling up the instruments on the portable sterilizer as she used them and pouring lotions for her. She was very gentle and very deft. Her thin hands were somehow like Dr. Clifford's—they almost seemed to be listening as they touched the men—as though her fingertips could detect the most microscopic cry of pain from the tissues she was handling.

When we came to Mr. Enderby she said, "There is nothing to do here. You are comfortable?"

"No," he told her. "Nicht comfortable. There's a crumb or something under the edge of my plaster. Be dears, and get it out, will you? It hurts like the devil."

We rolled him over. There was no crumb, but just below the edge of the plaster corset there was an ominous blue patch. Staff's eyelashes fluttered, and she looked at me. "You recognize what this is, nurse?"

"A bruise?"

She touched it gently. It was not elastic at all, and the skin dragged back slowly from her fingers. "No. Not a bruise. You have been taught differently from that. No?" She reached for the spirit bottle and poured some into her hand. "The soap, please, nurse." I passed it to her, and she made a lather with the soap and spirit in her palm, and began to rub it into the blue gray mark. "You see what I do, nurse? You do this every hour for this man. Mr. Enderby, you remind, please, if the nurses forget?"

"Sure. What is it?"

Then it dawned on me. "Is it a—"

Staff frowned and I stopped. You didn't have to tell patients they had the beginnings of a bedsore. It was a dreadful disgrace.

"A pressure mark," I amended it. "That's all." I saw how it could have happened, too. Peta hadn't rubbed it when she did the beds. Noble had left it to Peta. The night people hadn't looked because he hadn't complained. It was easily done, if just one person slipped up.

Back by the table staff said, "This is a bad thing, nurse, you understand? You will be careful with the treatment? Every hour. I have to report this to matron. This is the rule."

"Why, staff?"

"I do not know. This is the rule. Bedsores must be reported in every case. Also the heads which are—which are—what is it we say?"

"Infested? Pediculous?"

"That is right. Pediculous. We report these things before the relatives do so. You see? Because they are our shame when they come after a patient is admitted."

"I see," I said. "So somebody will be in trouble over Mr. Enderby?"

She nodded soberly. "We will all be so unless it quickly is better."

So it was just too bad that I forgot all about rubbing Nigel Enderby's back again until after tea. Now I have to report to matron in the morning and explain why I did, and I simply don't know. Only the visitors kept me so busy, putting flowers in water and answering questions, that it went clean out of my head. I shall never make a nurse. Poor mother must be turning in her grave.

March 1

AT NINE O'CLOCK I joined the line outside matron's office and tried to look nonchalant. I expect everyone else was trying to do the same, but none of them seemed to be having very much success. I was at the far end of the line opposite the R.M.O.'s office, and while I stood there against the wall Mr. Blunt came past.

He swung around after he passed and smiled. "Dropped any good drums lately?" he wanted to know. "Who've you decapitated this time?"

I shook my head. "Nobody. It's—" And then I remembered that Nigel Enderby knew him and closed my lips again firmly.

"Well? It's what?"

"You wouldn't understand," I said. "Much too technical. But a man in Ward 7 says he's a friend of yours. I suppose you know he's there? His name's Enderby."

"Lord, yes. Nig Enderby. I'm glad you told me—I've been meaning to go up and see the blighter—I forgot all about it." So I was not the only one who forgot things. "Tell him I'll be up tomorrow, will you?" He grinned. "Good luck with the matron."

"Thanks," I said. "I expect I shall need it."

But after all matron was quite nice about it, in a stern kind of way. She explained all about bedsores, all over again, and said she knew they didn't look much, especially when they were only just beginning like this one, but that they were terribly important things not to have in one's ward.

I said, "Yes, matron. Thank you, matron. I'm sorry."

She relaxed then and sat back in her swivel chair. "How are you liking the wards, nurse?"

"Very much, thank you, matron."

"Remember, nurse—there is never any need to worry. There is always someone senior to whom you can go. Never act on your own initiative unless you are quite sure that what you are doing is the right thing." She leaned forward with her long white hands on her desk, and I hid my red ones behind my back. "Even I have to do that sometimes, nurse, you know. There is nothing to be ashamed of in taking orders and seeking advice. Even I have to ask the Management Committee what I should do, sometimes. Remember that."

"Yes, matron." I looked up. "May I go now?"

"You may, nurse. When is your off duty today?"

I remembered that Sister Harrowby had exchanged only two words with me so far. And that they had been, "You—half day." So I said, "It's my half day, Matron."

"I see. You are going home to Wylde Green, are you?"

I said I wasn't—that father was in Liverpool, and I hadn't yet decided how to spend my free time.

"Then I hope you'll get some fresh air, nurse. Try to get out every day, whatever the weather." She turned around and looked out of the window, and I had time to admire the beautiful gophered frill of her cap. "And the weather isn't going to provide any excuses today. Look at the sun. The frost has quite gone."

So when I got to the home and found my golf clubs waiting for me, there wasn't any problem at all. They had been in home sister's office since Friday, she said, and she had meant to send them up to my room. Father had brought them, on his way to Liverpool.

I phoned his hotel, but he wasn't in, so I had to leave a message for him to say that I'd call again tomorrow.

Home sister has just been in again. This time my light has to be out in one minute.

MATRON CAN SAY what she likes—it is pouring with rain, and I am not going out at any price. I still have Monday's diary to catch up on.

After I'd tried to call father, I went upstairs and changed into a flannel skirt and my suede jacket, and ferreted out my golf shoes. I was just polishing them when Braich-Jones came in to borrow a pair of nylons. That's two pairs she has of mine. I can't think why she doesn't buy some of her own.

She said, "Going out?"

I was tempted to say that nothing of the sort had crossed my mind and that I was just polishing my spikes to occupy myself. But Braich-Jones is too thick-skinned to react to that kind of thing. She'd most likely believe it. "Yes," I said. "I thought I might have a game of golf."

"You must be mad," she told me. "Surely your feet won't stand up to that, will they?"

I shrugged. "I don't know yet. I'm willing to try it. Matter of fact, it might do them good. A spot of springy turf will be a nice change after polished floors."

"Where are you going? Harbone?"

"Not likely. Not when I can get to my own club. It'll take me an hour or more, but it's worth it."

"Where do you go, then?" She settled on the end of my bed, as though she proposed to stay all afternoon.

I told her I had every intention of getting out toward Lichfield, to the Whittington course. "It's always dry, whatever the weather," I explained. "This frost won't have put any of our greens out of commission."

"Sooner you than me," she commented. She got up from the bed again. "Reason I asked is that I saw someone else just barging off with golf clubs. Thought it might be a put-up job between you."

"Who?" If one of the others was going, I reflected, I

wouldn't mind playing somewhere nearby instead. After all, there might not be anyone at Whittington to give me a game—I was quite resigned to going around on my own or with the pro. "One of the nurses?"

Braich-Jones put on one of her mysterious Welsh looks—it's done by narrowing the eyes and breathing rather heavily—and said, "No. Not one of the nurses," and waited to be coaxed. For once I didn't bother, and by the time my spikes looked like chestnuts again she had wandered away.

I was lucky with the buses, and I was out at Whittington by shortly after three o'clock. There was a mixed foursome just moving off, and one of them, the secretary's wife, waved to me. "If we'd known you were coming," she called, "we'd have arranged something. Chap in the clubhouse might give you a game." She pointed to the lounge windows. "He's a doctor. You may have something in common."

I left my clubs by the front door and went into the lounge. There was a tall man leaning on the bar counter in the corner, talking to the steward, with his back to me.

"That's right, sir," the steward said. "He said he was very, very sorry, but he was operating on an emergency case, and he couldn't get here until five o'clock, sir. Those were his very words, sir."

"Confound him," said a quiet voice that I knew quite well already. I began to retreat, but it was too late. The steward was looking at me.

"Young lady here might like to give you nine holes while you wait, sir. Miss Elliot."

I was still in the middle of pulling an appalling face at Robert when Dr. Clifford turned around.

It hadn't occurred to me that he wouldn't instantly recognize me as one of the nurses he'd seen in the children's ward. But he didn't. We must all look very much alike, I suppose, and he sees so many of us. He smiled gently and said, "Good afternoon. You let down, too?"

I'm sure I was the color of matron's crimson carpet. "No," I got out somehow. "I—I just came on speculation." Then I remembered my manners as a member. "You wouldn't care for a few holes while you wait, would you?"

"Very much," he said. He stood up straight and stopped leaning on the counter, and he was about two feet taller than the steward. "Can you face it?"

I wanted to fall right through the floor. "I'm only a rabbit," I warned him. "Fourteen handicap."

"That's hardly rabbithood from the ladies' scores," he said kindly. "I'm a poor nine myself. I'll give you a stroke a hole if you like."

I was indignant. "Indeed you won't!" I protested. "I'll have one on the long holes, where I'm due for them, thank you. *And* I'll go off the back tees."

His eyebrows went up, and his gray eyes were laughing. "As you wish. I'll just change my shoes, and I'll be with you. My name's Clifford."

"Dr. Clifford," the steward said breathily, "was expecting to meet our Dr. Coombes, you know, Miss Elliot."

I knew Dr. Coombes. What he was doing operating on an emergency case I couldn't imagine because he has a large country practice, and the nearest he ever gets to an operating room is when he gives anesthetics at the Lichfield hospital occasionally. The steward must have made a mistake.

"I see," I said. "I'll see you on the first tee in five minutes, then, Dr. Clifford."

Up in the ladies' lounge I powdered my hot face and tried to make my hair respectable. I loathe wearing hats, and my hair looked pretty windswept. Peta's hair is always so tidy, and in any case a blond can afford to be windswept, but mine has always behaved like a blacking brush, and it will never lie down quietly. That's why I keep it short, even though father does think it looks unfeminine. If I let it grow I should look like one of those unkempt Italian film stars: I would rather have it boyish and moderately controllable, although it is very difficult to make my caps stay on.

When I went out and crossed the road to the first tee, he was already there, practicing his swing. He had a very good swing, too. It looked as though it would get results—unlike mine, which looks definitely stylish, but the ball is apt to trickle about thirty yards and then fade.

"Your honor," I said. "You're a visitor."

He didn't argue. It was a beautiful drive, right up the middle of the fairway, in line with the pin. I had to cut the top off mine, of course, out of sheer nerves.

"Take it again," he suggested.

I frowned. "No, thanks. I'm out of practice, that's all."

"I said take it again," he said mildly. He put a fresh ball down for me. "I'm a visitor, remember; I have to have my own way."

Before I drove he put his hand gently over mine. "Left hand a bit higher," he told me. "That's it. Now, keep your head down this time."

He was right, too. My ball flew after his and lay only about twenty yards short of it.

"You see?" he said. "Now if you'd gone off the ladies' tee, instead of being tough, you'd have been level, wouldn't you?"

That's the way it was, all the way around. He lectured me in the bunker on the second, chivvied me along the third and made me take my chip shot again on the fifth. By the time we were going down the cathedral hole, he was only a hole ahead of me. And I had more confidence than I'd had for ages.

And then, below the green, I saw Dr. Coombes's car drawn up on the rough. I looked at my watch. The time had flown past because it was nearly five o'clock. As I took my putt I realized that I was in a spot. Dr. Coombes was sure to come across to us, and he was sure to know that I was at Tim's. My hand jerked, and the ball rolled feebly past the hole.

"And again," Dr. Clifford said. He brought my ball back. "Keep your wrists still, just use your arms as a pendulum, this time." I holed it.

Watching Dr. Coombes out of the corner of my eye, getting out of his car, I said desperately, "Look—there's something I have to tell you—" I looked up at Dr. Clifford. ". . . sir," I added.

"Yes?" He picked his own ball out of the can and replaced the flag. "What is it?" He stood with his hands on his hips, and I noticed how his eyes reflected the blue of his windbreaker, so that they were no longer plain gray at all. He had very dark lashes, too.

"I—I've been playing with you under false pretenses, sir," I said. "I'm Nurse Elliot. From the children's ward, you know, at St. Timothy's. You don't have to play with me ever again. I quite understand."

"Hush, girl," he said amiably. "I knew that. I thought you were going to confess that you played off scratch or something!"

"You—you knew, sir?" I was astonished. He hadn't said a word all the way around.

"Of course. It's my job to be observant, you know. But it wasn't relevant, was it? We're both off duty. You don't call me 'sir' out here, my dear. I have quite enough of being 'sir' when I'm working. Or didn't that ever occur to you?" He smiled, and when he did that all the haggard lines seemed to melt away. "No, I suppose it wouldn't. You're too young."

"Nearly twenty," I said. "And here's Dr. Coombes.

I'd better go in and you two can play together, sir—I mean Dr. Clifford.''

"Rubbish. You'll play around with us." He waved his club and called Dr. Coombes over. "Come on, slacker. Emergency operation, indeed!"

Dr. Coombes puffed across the rough and climbed the bank. "Why, hello, Lucy! Couldn't see who you were from the road. How's it going?" And before I could answer him he went on, "Well, so it was an emergency operation. Sent the result in to Tim's now, too."

"Give us the tools and we'll finish the job, eh?" Dr. Clifford sauntered across to the eighth tee and stamped the turf down, "What have you been up to, then?"

"Had to do an amputation. Did I sweat! Haven't done one since I was a resident. Anyway, you can get him patched up over there, I suppose."

"Why St. Tim's? No beds at Lichfield?"

"Nary a one to be had. This fellow was working in the quarry, out on the Coleshill Road—one of these earthmover gadgets fell on top of him. Terrible mess. Couldn't do anything else—it was just a tangled mass of machinery. The district nurse helped me, and that was it."

Dr. Clifford stuck a scarlet tee in the turf. "Good man, Bill. Dinsmore'll tidy him up for you, I expect. It's his take-in day."

We played the last holes without talking much, except that the two men talked shop about patients I had never heard of. And about every ten strokes Dr. Clifford came over to me and checked my grip. I was doing much better than I used to. Just shifting my left hand made all the difference. I must really keep on trying that; it gives the ball real zing.

We all had tea together when we got in. What our steward calls "tea" is a thing that happens anytime up to eight o'clock and consists of ham and eggs and sausages, and as many cakes as we can eat. I don't know how he does it at the price. Dr. Coombes paid the bill and wouldn't hear of my chipping in. Then he said, "Do you have to get back to hospital, Lucy?"

"Yes. I'm going on the bus." I smiled. "I know it's your half-day—you don't have to offer me a lift."

"I'll take you," Dr. Clifford said laconically.

"But you don't go back to hospital, sir. Do you?"

"No. True. But I can easily take you."

"But—" I stopped. How could I explain to him how people would talk if I rolled up to the home in a consultant's car? "Very well," I said. "Thank you very much."

I needn't have worried. He obviously knows all about it. Because when we came to the corner above the home he stopped the car and said, "I expect you'd rather take it from here."

It wasn't until afterward that it occurred to me that he didn't want to be seen with me.

CHAPTER THREE

SISTER HARROWBY has a great many unpleasant little ways, so that although she is not very vocal her general nuisance rating is still fairly high. One of her infuriating habits is to hold back our mail until we are going to lunch break. Any other ward sister dishes out the nurses' letters with the patients', when she brings them back after her morning trip down to matron's office. Some of them simply leave them in the kitchen, to be picked up, or place them on the ward table, but mostly (Greta's word for it) they are handed over personally. But not in Ward 7.

When Sister Harrowby comes back from the office she takes her time distributing letters and parcels to the patients, and even if anyone reports at that time, before going over to the home, she makes no attempt to fish behind her apron bib for the staff mail that anyone can clearly see opaquely bulging there. She thinks about this only when she decides to roll up her sleeves and do a few dressings—and she probably wouldn't think of it then, except for the fact that she keeps her dressing frills behind her bib, too, and can't very well extricate them without also unloading the letters.

This morning I watched her for half an hour, pottering about the ward with a telltale bulge on her flat bosom, before I said, "May I go off duty now, sister?"—and looked meaningly at her bib.

"You may. And don't be late back. There are two Winchesters of saline to bring up from the dispensary, so allow time for it, nurse." No attempt whatever to go through the letters. She simply went on counting out packets of gauze from the stock cupboards as though I didn't exist.

"Are there—are there any letters for me, sister?"

She slapped down the parcel she was holding. "Really, nurse! You can see I'm counting!" She began all over again on the pile of little blue rolls.

It was twenty-past ten before she finally locked the cupboard again and condescended to sort the mail. She put down two letters on the marble slab in silence and then said sharply, "You were supposed to go off at ten, Nurse Elliot. Unpunctuality is as bad one way as the other. Don't let it happen again."

How can you argue with anyone like that?

But at last I have managed to read Peta's note and father's long letter. Peta's is very short, and she sounds dumpish, but there is a P.S. which reads, "Have asked—doesn't repay." Bang go two pair of nylons, obviously. Next time I shall have only one pair left to my name.

Father's letter was much longer. He says the Liverpool job is going well and that he has been talking to some of the nurses. They tell him that Tim's is a cracking good training school, and that I am lucky to get a vacancy here so soon. I suppose that's meant to encourage me on my prickly path. But the interesting thing is that although I was joking when I said, "You'd better design some extension for St. Timothy's," father has just heard that our Management Committee is exercising itself on the question of extensions—and that there is to be a competitive thing over a new Outpatients Department. He doesn't say whether his is going to enter a design, but I imagine that is what he means. So if I can't achieve much by my own efforts, it may yet be possible to reap a little reflected glory as the daughter of Robert Verney Elliot—"you know, the architect for the new O.P.D., of course." And that, after being only junior probationer on Ward 7, will be a nice change.

Of course, after being late coming off the ward, and then spending a lot of time on these wild dreams and on writing back to father and Peta, I forgot all about allowing time to call at the dispensary, and at half-past twelve I was scuttling along the tunnel with a heavy winchester under each arm. (I can't think what Sister Harrowby—or anyone else—does with all these gallons of saline solution, though I do know it is used for giving intravenous drips with and so on. Also, that Sister Harrowby has old-fashioned ideas about wet dressings and likes to use it mixed with Eusol on septic wounds. But even so, it seems to me that I cart about an inordinate amount of the stuff. Maybe somebody is addicted to it, the way people get addicted to drugs? But there wouldn't be much point—like sea water, all it would do for a person would be to make them sick, if they drank enough of it.)

Just where the tunnel emerges into the ground floor corridor I ran into Mr. Blunt. I would. He said, "What—again? I suppose you think I'm going to carry that up to the children's ward for you this time?"

I tried to look dignified. "Not at all," I told him. "I'm not on the children's ward, for one thing. And for another, I'm quite capable of carrying the stuff myself." I pushed past him.

"I'm sure you are." He lifted one of the heavy bottles out of my grasp. "But I'd hate to see you drop one in your enthusiasm. Lead on—where are you now?" He turned around and prepared to go back to the wards. "Oh I know. Ward 7. Nig Enderby was telling me about you."

I gave in and led the way back to the ward block. "What did he tell you? That Sister Harrowby and I are as one? Or that my hands are as cold as kippers? Nothing complimentary, I'll be bound."

"That," he informed me gently, "is known as fishing. So my lips are sealed. Wild horses won't—"

"Good morning, Blunt," said Dr. Clifford's quiet voice, just behind us. And then he added, "Good morning, Lucy," as casually as though he had been saying, "Spatula, nurse."

I gulped in amazement, and I saw Buster's dark eyebrows go up, before I mumbled, "Good morning, sir."

He took the other winchester out of my hands. "May I?"

He couldn't have known what a spot he was putting me in. For one thing nurses are taught that they must wait on the consultants, not the reverse; for another, we are not encouraged to talk to the men in any case—and to be trotting along between two of them was unheard of. Worst of all, I was already five minutes late, and now I should be later still, if I had to go at his slow relaxed pace instead of hurrying. There were four flights of stairs up to Ward 7, and I was very conscious of Sister Harrowby fuming away at the top of them.

"Sir," I protested. "I have to hurry. Please—I—can—"

He looked down at me calmly. "Ward 7, isn't it?" I wondered how he knew that. "Very well. We'll take the elevator."

"But we're not allowed to use the elevator, sir," I said desperately. "Except with patients. At least—" I felt my face turning raspberry pink. "At least I'm not allowed to, sir. You are, of course."

"Hush," he said, the way he had said it on the golf course. "You worry too much, Nurse Elliot. Come with me." He took the other winchester from Buster and nodded to him. "You get down to that clinic of mine,

Blunt. There's a queue waiting as it is. I'll be with you shortly."

When we reached the elevator I opened the gates, closed them again and pressed the fourth-floor button. "Sister will be furious," I told him. "I forgot all about allowing time to go to the dispensary and—"

"You mean you have to do this on your own time?" His eyes opened wide reflecting the dull blue of his tie.

"Why, yes, sir! It's the practice."

"And how much off duty have you had?"

"Technically, two-and-a-half hours, sir. But not actually, because of waiting for the letters and so on." I found myself explaining why I had been late going off. It was only as we emerged from the elevator, at the end of the flat, that it dawned on me that I was telling tales out of school to a member of the Management Committee. I said, "I oughtn't to have told you that. So please forget it, sir. It slipped out. I wasn't complaining."

"I'm sure you weren't. I won't give you away." He sailed on ahead of me straight through the swing doors, before I could even open them for him, and dumped the winchesters on sister's table. And then he made a bee-line for Staff Haarstein. Sister wasn't in sight. (I don't know what he said to staff, but she hasn't said a word about my being late. Nor has sister—if she ever knew.) He smiled at me as he went out, and I rolled up my sleeves and began to collect the dishes the men had used and came down to earth again.

While Noble and I were straightening the beds ready for visiting hours she looked at me curiously. "Friend of yours?"

"Who?"

"Dr. Clifford. Who else? You didn't think I meant this specimen, did you?" She grinned down at Nigel Enderby as we stripped off his rumpled bedspread.

"Unfair to Enderby," he complained. "Me, I'm every

nurse's friend. Ward 7's little ray of sunshine, I am."

We heaved him over and rubbed his back. "All better," I observed. "Not a mark. All that fuss—" I frowned at him as we tucked him in again.

"Dr. Clifford," Noble repeated patiently. "You know him?"

"Slightly," I said. "I think he's spoken to me on two occasions." I plumped up Nigel Enderby's pillow. "Why?"

"Silent type, then. Quiet ride, was it?" Noble's eyes twinkled. "If you will ride about in that great car of his—lucky for you I was the only one who saw you, my girl."

"I see," I said. "Spies in the camp. Well, he only gave me a lift. Why not?"

"Why not indeed? I'm all for a full life. Only thing is, it was a good thing our vivacious staff didn't see you." She bent down to ram the locker cloth into the cupboard, and when she straightened up again I was still staring at her.

Out in the bathroom I said, "Say that again."

"What?" She stopped folding a sheet and looked at me. "I said it was a good thing Staff Haarstein didn't see you, that's all. What's wrong?"

"Yes, but why?"

Noble's dark eyes were suddenly very wide open. "Why—she might get the idea that your mind wasn't on our work. What else?"

I let my breath out, then. "Nothing," I said.

"Goodness me—" She smiled over the lid of the laundry basket. "Whatever gave you *that* idea?"

March 7

IT IS CONSIDERED rather a good thing to be off duty on Sundays from lunch until 5:30 P.M. It breaks the day up. Certainly it is an opportunity to have a hot bath without the continual bangings on the door that spoil the process night and morning. And on Sundays the heating is stepped up in our rooms, for some reason. Probably because the laundry isn't at work, and the home gets the benefit of the spare steam. So most people who are off duty in the afternoon never go out at all but stay lazing in their bedrooms, reading, or writing letters, and that is what I have been doing.

I have finished a long screed to Peta. There was plenty to tell her. For one thing I copied out the notice that was posted in the common room last night. It says:

> The Hospital Management Committee has directed that in future off-duty periods will be times from the actual time of leaving wards or departments, and no duties, missions or lectures shall be undertaken except in duty periods unless in case of emergency. The committee has also arranged for staff mail to be delivered direct to the nurses' home as from Monday next.

Braich-Jones was with me when I read it, and to cover up the fact that I was hot and cold all over I said, "What's the betting that Sister 'Gorgon' will declare a state of emergency, as from now?"

And then I realized that when Dr. Clifford said, "I won't give you away" he probably meant it. I don't think he is the kind to break his word, even though I did wonder for a mad moment whether he was the kind to fall for anyone as inarticulate as Staff Haarstein. (And after all, what she lacks in personality, she makes up in being a wonderful nurse. No doubt in Norwegian she is tremendously vital, a regular little chatterbox.) But how was I to know that the committee met on Friday evening? Or that he took me so seriously?

I would have liked to tell Braich-Jones, but she is really

o substitute for Peta, so I told her the bit about his arrying the saline for me in a devious kind of way, by irst asking what it was all used for and why.

She explained about istopic saline and normal saline nd how it was a sort of substitute blood on occasion, nd then she said, "He was R.M.O. when Greta began er training." I thought it wouldn't be long before we ad a quote from Greta. "Very much the ladies' man, he says, But he's changed since he became a consultant. Goodness, when he comes to Ward 2 we don't get two vords out of him. Talk about strong and silent—"

"Ward 2?" I said quickly. "But I thought he was a ediatrician, simply."

"Lord, no. He's good with kids—but he does adult earts mostly."

That explained his listening fingers.

March 11

MUST HAVE BEEN mad to think that anything whatever ould make Ward 2 a more livable place. After three ays of it, I take back all I have ever said against Braich-ones. She is a heroine of the first water if this is what he has put up with for nearly a month without com-laining.

Sister Tutor seems to have decided that Braich-Jones as had enough medicine at Fevers and ought to get more urgery in, and prevailed upon matron to swap us over.

"It's only fair," Braich-Jones said. "All the surgery 've ever seen has been the odd tracheotomy. Anyhow, ou don't like Ward 7—so it suits you."

I glowed inwardly at the thought of seeing Dr. Clif-ord and Buster instead of Dr. Welby and his dreary lit-e woman H.S. on round days. "But I don't like all hese changes," I complained. "Other people don't ave them."

"They do. Often. And there's the big change soon—we all move then."

"When's that?"

"Some time before quarter day, Greta says. She's going to the operating room, the lucky creature. Wish I was."

I didn't much care where Greta went: it only mattered to me that I was going to Dr. Clifford's ward. No sister could be as bad as Sister Heywood-Bence was reputed to be, with a man like him to work for, I thought. (I now wonder what on earth she might be if she worked for anyone else.)

The very first thing she did was to send me to matron for "wasting time in chatting familiarly to housemen."

That is an exaggeration. It was houseman, singular; I wasn't chatting, he was; and I wasn't wasting time, because I was working while he did it. The first time Buster Blunt came into the ward was when I'd been there approximately an hour. Sister had just come on duty and was taking the night report. I was madly slapping cups and saucers onto the trolley in the kitchen because in Ward 2 the drinks have to be laid before the ward is tidied for rounds. (This way, I gather, the beds keep tidier longer, and the ward maid—the abominable Agnes—has longer in which to polish the floor. A good many things in Ward 2 are arranged to suit Agnes and not for any other sensible reason.)

He put his head into the kitchen when he saw me and said, "Hi Lucy!" That was all. He evidently thought that if it was all right for his chief to use my Christian name, it was all right for him, too. And, of course, he was probably surprised to see me there. Sister—whose ears are quite unlike anyone else's because she can literally hear through brick walls and around corners—shot out of the ward and stood glaring at the pair of us.

"So this is how you waste your time, is it, Nurse Elliot?" she barked. "No wonder you had to be moved from Ward 7 and the children's ward. Now I understand! You can see matron. If you think the doctors are here to flirt with you, you're mistaken. As for you, Mr. Blunt, you ought to know better!''

Buster didn't turn a hair. "Yes, sister. Sorry, sister," he said serenely. ''My fault.'' He vanished into the ward, swinging his stethoscope and smiling to himself.

She went on looking at me, with her hands on her hips and her red face screwed up in temper. ''You heard what I said, Nurse Elliot? You go to matron at nine o'clock.''

"Yes, sister.'' I went on looking at the blue cups and saucers until I heard the doors slap together again.

I couldn't imagine what I was going to say to matron when I got there. I would have to cross that bridge when I came to it. All I could do was to put on a clean apron and do my best to make my hair lie flat in front instead of sticking up like a cockscomb.

I trembled my way across to her desk when she said, ''Come in,'' and stood there with my hands behind my back.

At last she looked up from the passes she was signing. ''Ah, yes, Nurse Elliot.'' She smiled in the feline way of hers. ''I sent for you because I wanted to have a word with you about Nurse Royde. I believe you are old friends?''

I couldn't say anything for a moment, and then I managed to mumble, ''You sent for me, matron? I—I thought—'' And then I swallowed and pulled myself together enough to say, ''Yes, matron. We were at school together.'' I could cheerfully have strangled Sister Heywood-Bence if she had popped up from behind matron's desk at that moment.

''Good. Now it seems that she's making quite good progress, as far as the diphtheria is concerned. But they are a little worried because she isn't recovering her spirits. She seems to be worrying about something.''

She looked at me inquiringly, with her head on one side. "I thought you might be able to help me, perhaps?"

"Of course, matron. If I can."

She picked up her paperweight and looked at it with great interest. It was once a table lighter, but the working parts have been filed off, and, in any case matron doesn't smoke, and it is generally assumed that she keeps it on her desk because it is a replica of one of those Aladdin lamps people always associate with nursing. (Also, of course, it would be a handy missile if anyone tried anything.) It is said that when she plays with it, it is a sign that she has something to say and doesn't know how to put it. So I waited patiently while she fiddled with it. It was a pleasant change to see someone else being inarticulate.

After a moment or two she put it down sharply and said, "Yes, well. Do you know what is worrying Nurse Royde?"

"Not really, matron. I could guess—but I might be wrong."

"Guess away, nurse. It may be helpful."

"I think she may be worrying about coming back, matron."

"Oh? Why?"

I hunted for words. "Well, she began on a male ward, and—she took it rather hard. She's an orphan, and she hasn't had an ordinary sort of upbringing and—" I fumbled for a way to put it.

Matron nodded understandingly. "I understand, nurse. She was a little nervous?"

"Yes, matron. Shy, you know."

"Quite. Yes. Anything else?"

It was no use. I had to tell her what I thought. "Matron—I don't think that's all. I could be wrong, of course, but—I think, honestly, that she doesn't want to go on with nursing, and she's too proud to say so."

She sat back in her chair and wound her fingers

together in a tight knot. "Not go on with nursing? But, nurse, she had hardly begun." She rubbed her forehead incredulously. "You really think she had decided that already on the strength of a few days in one ward?"

"I think she may have. You see, matron, she tells me most things, and if it were anything else I think I'd know. But she wouldn't say much if it were that, because, well—she may have come here rather more to do as I did than because she had an original urge to come. If you see what I—"

"I see, nurse. She is fond of you, and she looks on you as a kind of relative, and she might try to carry on against her inclinations rather than feel she had let you down?"

"That's it, matron," I said gratefully.

Her mouth twitched. "I see. She must be very fond of you, nurse. You think, then, that if she was not expected to come back, she wouldn't be so anxious?"

"Yes, matron. But you see I may be wrong, and she might settle if she had a chance to begin on the children's ward or something. So it wouldn't do to assume anything."

She began to play with the ex-lighter again. This time when she put it down she said, "You have relieved my mind, nurse. You see, there's no question of Nurse Royde beginning again—either in the children's ward or anywhere else in this hospital. I had been wondering whether it was going to increase her depression when I told her that. Now I see that it won't."

"She can't begin again, matron? But why?"

"Because, nurse, although I told you she was making good progress, what I did not tell you was that there have been kidney complications. And those can be quite serious, as you realize." (I did not, but it was not the moment to say so, so I nodded wisely.) "Nurse Royde will be able to take up other work, of course, but the doctors think that nursing will impose an unnecessary strain. So, you see—'' She spread her hands eloquently. ''The problem is half-solved, if she is not going to grieve, isn't it?''

I said that was how it appeared and that I was sorry. Then I said, ''I didn't know that was why you wanted to see me, matron. I came because sister told me to report to you for—for wasting time talking to Mr. Blunt.''

''Dear me! And did you, nurse?''

I described the encounter to her.

''I see. Well, nurse, I don't think we need punish you for that, do you? But you know, I don't want any of you young nurses to become engrossed in—in friendships during your training. A nurse's life is a hard one, even since the Rushcliffe Committee came along! And you need all your energies and attention free to concentrate on your training. Don't you?''

''Yes, matron.''

''That is why we have rules about not chattering to housemen and why I don't care to allow too many late passes. It isn't to make your lives miserable, though you may think so, some of you. It's to help you to get on with your work. You understand?''

''Yes, matron. Thank you, matron.''

She dabbed down the paperweight with a final little thud. ''Then you may go, nurse. Thank you for giving me your opinion. Tell sister I kept you, and then she will understand why you are late back from your lunch break.''

After that, I naturally took my time. It was the first time I had turned my mattress for nearly a week, had home sister but known. And I had two cups of coffee instead of one, while I thought about Peta.

Braich-Jones was in the dining room, too. She waved when she saw me, and I threaded my way through the

tanding crowd around the hot plate where the coffee
ugs stood.

"Elliot! Message for you."

"Who from—Ruby? No, I haven't hidden her polish-
ng rags."

"Silly. No, from Mr. Enderby."

"Mr. Enderby. What about?"

She ferreted behind her bib. "Here—he sent you a note.
He's going home today, you know. Had his plaster off
yesterday, and he's fine. You must have made a conquest
r something." She watched beadily while I opened it.

It was very short. It just said:

Thanks for all you did for me. There's a box of
nylons coming along when I get home. I suppose
nines will be right? And Buster tells me your affec-
tions aren't otherwise engaged, as they say, so
what about an evening out sometime?

Nigel

Nothing wrong with that—except that there was no
ddress on it and no telephone number so that the bit
bout an evening out was just padding. "Thanks," I
aid. "It's just a thank-you-and-goodbye note." And I
dded, "By the way—don't bother to return those
ylons. I've plenty."

March 15

CAN'T REALLY BELIEVE that it's a fortnight since I had a
alf day off. Of course, I ought to have had a day off
ast week, but for some reason Sister Heywood-Bence
ad it all worked out that I wasn't entitled to one
ecause in her ward, as she says, things are worked out
n a monthly basis. This is idiotic, because it means that
's possible to work more than a week—and then spend

a fortnight waiting for a day with more than two-and-a-half hours off duty in it.

It doesn't seem two weeks since I played golf, either, but I suppose it must be. Life in Ward 2 is so crammed with action that the time goes past on oiled wheels. For one thing, it is perfectly true about women being more demanding than men. What's more, they have no sense of timing. Mrs. Garrell, our veteran, has this kind of thing developed to a fine art. Three times this morning I passed her bed, saw her look at me and then reached the other end of the ward, with my hands full, before she reacted.

The first time I heard the thin whine of, "Nurse, nurse!" just as I was leaning on the annex door to open it.

I went back. "Yes, Mrs. Garrell?"

She looked at me accusingly. "You knocked my newspaper down when you went past, nurse. I can't reach it."

"I'm sorry." I picked it up and gave it to her. "Is there anything else you want?"

She let her face droop in a martyred way. "No, thank you, nurse. Sorry to trouble you, I'm sure."

I raced back to pick up the back tray again.

This time it was an urgent squeak. "Nurse!"

I looked back over my shoulder. She was waving her hands frantically. "Yes, Mrs. Garrell? What is it?"

"Come here, nurse. I can't shout."

For the second time, I put the tray down on Miss Blumberg's bedside table, and for the second time she winked at me. When I reached Mrs. Garrell's bed by the ward door, she beckoned me close to her. "Nurse, what's for dinner today? Is it fish, because I—"

"I don't know, Mrs. Garrell. Is that all you wanted me for?"

Her fat, cream-colored face sagged again and tears came into her eyes. I am hardened by now to Mrs. Gar-

ell's tears. They are no more significant than the drips
from the bathroom tap. "That's all, nurse." She lay
back hopelessly on her pillows. "I don't want to bother
you, I'm sure."

"That's all right," I told her. "But if there's anything
else, tell me now—because I've a lot to do."

She shook her head and managed to give the impression that she was thoroughly cowed, and I went back
again and scampered into the bathroom before she
could open her mouth again. Instantly, sister burst
through the door after me. "Can't you hear Mrs. Gar-
ell calling you, nurse? Are you deaf or something?"

"I've just been to her, sister."

"Well, she wants you again. And for heaven's sake
hurry—you know Mr. Clifford's due at any monent,
and she's his first patient."

Back up the ward again. I could see from her face
what she wanted this time, without all the whispers behind her hand. And I had no sooner got the screens halfway around her than Dr. Clifford walked in, and sister
bundled me on one side and pulled down the bedclothes
for him. She very quickly jerked them up again. "Nurse
Elliot!" she bellowed. "I thought you were asked to at-
tend to this patient?"

"Yes, sister," I said. "I was just—"

"Then get on with it! Really, do you think Dr. Clifford has time to wait while you—"

He cleared his throat and tapped her shoulder. "My
fault, sister. I interrupted nurse at whatever she was doing. Let's get on, shall we?" He moved onto the next
bed, and I threw him a grateful look. Only he wasn't
noticing, which was a pity, because I am sure it was very
eloquent.

But he happened to finish his round a few moments
before Tinsley, our staff, who is quiet and inoffensive as
sister is the other thing, took us down to lunch; and as

we passed through the bottom corridor he was still there talking to Buster. So I handed him all my thanks again with a smile for good measure.

He touched my arm. "Just a moment, nurse."

I stopped as if I had air brakes. "Sir?"

"Tell her, Blunt. Tell her what I told you when you first had to deal with Sister Heywood-Bence. It may help her." His thin face was perfectly serious, but his voice had laughter in it.

Buster grinned. "The chief said, 'Remember, Blunt, she isn't a normal woman being difficult; she's a difficult woman being normal.' And he also told me that her blood pressure was a scandal. Does that help any?"

Funnily enough, it did. "Yes," I said. "Yes, I suppose it does. Thanks for the thought." And then I looked up at Dr. Clifford. "But if her blood pressure's a scandal, why does she go on working?"

He shrugged helplessly. "What makes you think anyone could stop her? Her blood pressure's been a hundred and eighty over a hundred ever since I've known her. And that's ever since I was a fifth-year student. You think I can do anything?" He gave me a little push. "On your way, Lucy."

He has a wonderful smile. It takes years off him.

I shall go and play golf now, and it won't matter if I go around quite alone because I shall do all the things he told me to do, and it will be just as though he were with me.

March 16

FATHER ALWAYS SAYS that my big fault is that I expect too much and look forward too much and build up disappointments for myself. I suppose he is right.

My half day didn't work out at all the way I meant it to. I was let in for a ladies' foursome, and nothing bores me more. Especially when one of them is Mrs. Coombes.

Halfway along the second fairway she said, "I won-der you dare show your face here. A good thing Bill isn't here—he might have something to say to you."

"To me? Why?" I scuffed my feet in the heather, looking for my ball. "What have I done?"

"Well, not you—" Mrs. Coombes dug out a large divot and left her ball sitting. "Not you, but your wretched hospital!"

When she had managed to get onto the green I said, 'What's Tim's done to Dr. Coombes?"

"Only killed off his patient. Isn't that enough?"

"Not—not the one he sent in from the quarry?" I could see how disappointed he would be, after sweating over the rescue work. "What a shame!"

We walked side by side across the green. "Do you know, Lucy, he was so fed up that he wouldn't come to the club this afternoon. There!"

"It's no use being like that," I said. "These things do happen. But I'm sorry, all the same. He'd worked so hard on him."

"Yes. And he took it very badly that David Clifford didn't let him know, I may tell you. He more or less put him in his care."

So his name is David. David. David Clifford.

"Oh, but he couldn't do that," I pointed out. "Dr. Clifford is a physician. He had nothing to do with the surgical side at all. He wouldn't even know."

Mrs. Coombes rattled her ball irritably into the can. "He should have made it his business to find out! It was the least he could do!"

I lost my temper then. I asked her if she had any con-ception of the amount of time Dr. Clifford put in or the number of patients he had to deal with or how conscien-tious he was, and then breath gave out.

Not only Mrs. Coombes, but Miss Petrie and Mrs. Lunt were staring at me, by the time I'd finished.

Mrs. Lunt sat down on the tee box. "Well," she said, "now that you've got all that off your chest, Lucy, perhaps you'll tell us when your father's coming back? High time he did, I think!"

I forgot all the things Dr. Clifford had told me about my left hand and topped my ball viciously. "I don't know," I said. "Why?"

"Because we want to know what he's doing about The Laurels, for one thing," Miss Petrie said. "It isn't sold yet, is it?"

"Not as far as I know." I put a fresh ball down and tried to hear his voice saying, "Take it again." I did hear it, and the ball flew straight. "There was some talk about the Conservative Club making him an offer, but I don't think it came to anything. You don't want it, do you?"

"No. But I know somebody who does. Tell your father, Lucy, when you see him."

And then the rain came down in solid gray sheets. None of us had raincoats, and by the time we got to the clubhouse we were drenched. I was still too angry with Mrs. Coombes to want to eat with her, so as soon as I'd changed I caught the next bus back to Birmingham. Ever since I've been lazing in my room.

Not such a wonderful half day, after waiting so long for it, but I expect it is entirely my own fault. Father is quite right.

I always said that if I ever had a son I would call him David. I would, too. It's a fine name.

Home sister will not be able to complain tonight. It's only half-past nine, but I'm going to put my light out now and go to bed. I admire Braich-Jones more than I used to, since I've been in Ward 2, but this is not one of the nights when I want to talk to her. I shall have a whole hour to lie in bed and think, before I need go to sleep.

CHAPTER FOUR

I FORGOT to give in my hygiene notes to Sister Tutor's office first thing this morning, and the deadline is 10:00 A.M. So I had to go back for them after coffee, and even though I ran all the way to the home and back, I was about two minutes late back at the ward.

Sister was waiting for me, of course, standing at the foot of Miss Blumberg's bed, stiff as a white pouter pigeon, but much less appealing.

"Where do you think you've been?" she demanded. "Chatting about the weather with the house physician? Or was it the house governor this time? What time do you think it is? And why hasn't Miss Blumberg had her inhalation?"

I repressed the impulse to answer, "Lunch, no, no, nine thirty-two how do I know?" and murmured, "I'm sorry, sister," as I slipped my cuffs off.

"I doubt it, Nurse Elliot. I doubt it very much!" Her eyes, I decided, trying to detach mself, were extraordinarily like Maud's, who lives in the field at the back of The Laurels. Maud is an elderly Large White, and it would be an understatement to say that her temper is uncertain. She has been reprieved for years because she became a family pet, but it seems hardly worth the trouble. Once in a fit of rage, she knocked the vicar over, and he says it was a very similar experience to one he had in the Camel

Corps in the first war, and that it is easy to see that the Gadarene swine must have been something of an awe-inspiring spectacle. "Get it at once!" barked "the gorgon."

"Very well, sister," I said. "Thank you, sister." I went in search of the inhaler, the tinct, benzoin and the menthol crystals.

As Miss Blumberg's dark head dived under the big towel into the acrid steam she said, "How do you stand her—" The rest was muffled, but it sounded pretty venomous. And Mrs. Cottar in the next bed nodded sympathetically.

"So rude," she concurred primly. "You were very restrained, Nurse Elliot. What's the secret?" She looked up inquiringly and put down her paperback novel. "Don't you itch to answer back?"

I shrugged. "What do you think? But it wouldn't get me anywhere, would it? Besides—" I told her what Buster had said about sister's being a difficult woman and about her hypertension.

Miss Blumberg popped out of her bath towel, bright eyed. "Rubbish! That isn't what's insulating you this morning. There's a glint in your eyes. Good news?"

I felt pink all over. Miss Blumberg has a dark and penetrating gaze that misses very little. And she is a schoolteacher, and they always inhibit me. "Not specially," I told her. "I did get a present, though." I smiled. "Six pairs of nylons!" And as I set about the weekly task of picking fluff from the bed castors with a safety pin and cleaning the rubber tires with ether meth., I told her and Mrs. Cottar about the letter I've had from Nigel Enderby.

This time his address and telephone number are on the paper. He lives only about three minutes' walk from our new flat, just around the corner in Highbridge Road. The letter is only short, but it says:

...and about that evening I promised myself; I'm looking forward to that immensely. Trouble is, I'm not yet allowed to dance or anything, so it will have to be a sedentary business. Any ideas? I'll phone you on Wednesday evening and see how you are fixed for off duty.

And today is Wednesday.

I did not realize until I opened the parcel and saw his big scrawling handwriting how much I had wanted to hear from him. I know that we are strictly forbidden to pursue friendships with patients and ex-patients, but when I think of Nigel's cheerful grin and his tumbled mop of red hair, I know that I need his company if I am to see Ward 2 in perspective; and the rules seem fairly unimportant compared with the importance of keeping my balance. I have been very lonely without Peta.

This afternoon "the gorgon" was mercifully off duty, and when she had flounced off the ward staff called Noble and Marshall and me, and said, "Now—how about earning some ticks for your crosspapers?"

On our teaching charts—popularly known as "crosspapers"—we get a tick beside every process of nursing that we have had demonstrated to us and another tick, to make it into a cross, when we have satisfactorily done it by ourselves. We have to get a certain number of crosses before we can take our preliminary state exam, and the whole lot before we can sit our finals. The ward sisters are supposed to teach us these things, but some are more helpful than others, and some leave it all to their staff nurses. Tinsley is a gold medalist and will soon have a ward of her own. She is very keen on teaching, so "the gorgon" lets her get on with it.

I said, "I've only one, so far—assisting with dressings. Sister Tutor will take a dim view of that, if I don't get more before I hand my chart in before the change."

Staff nodded. "You haven't long to collect some, then—the change is next Sunday. What about you, Noble?" Noble said she hadn't done any trolley settings at all except en. saps, and Marshall, who is well on in her second year, complained that she had never yet been allowed to do a stomach washout or a nasal feed. "I've had the ticks for ages," she grumbled, "and I just can't get them crossed."

Tinsley frowned. "Well, I can't do much about that. We haven't a gastric in the ward, right now. Tell you what—" her small mouth curved up at the corner "—you could give me one. I'm game. Like to try?"

"Give you one?" Marshall was flabbergasted. "You mean, you'd let me?"

"Yes, if you're really so desperate. I don't mind suffering in the cause of science. But it will mean that you and Elliot, Noble, will have to take charge— I can't come charging out of the bathroom with a Ryle's tube in my tum, if anyone comes. All right?"

We said yes we would cope, and she went on, "Then before we get down to it I'll set a few trays for these two, Marshall, and they can be learning the setting while we're at it."

She showed us both how to set for lumbar puncture, aspiration and nutrient enemata, and gave us ticks for them; and explained about tepid sponges, hot packs and cold packs, before she and Marshall disappeared into the annex with their funnels and tubes to practice gastric lavage.

Most of the patients were napping before tea, and we sat at sister's table writing down the settings in our trolley books, before beginning on the bread and butter. When Mrs. Garrell called out that her hot-water bottle was cold, Noble said, "I'll go. She's my end of the ward." So that when Dr. Clifford and Buster walked in I was alone at the table.

I jumped to my feet. Buster said, "Are you in charge, nurse? Good gracious, how you girls grow up! Isn't Nurse Tinsley on duty?"

"Yes," I said. "But she's—she's in the middle of a tummy washout, Dr. Blunt. I can ask her—"

"No need," Dr. Clifford said. "We just want to do a lumbar puncture on the new girl—Miss Harris you know. I want a specimen of C.S.F. in a hurry. Can do?"

Flustered, I remembered that there was a tray already set for lumbar puncture, and that it was only a question of putting screens around Miss Harris and standing by. "Yes," I agreed. "Of course, sir."

I screened her off and explained what they were going to do, and remembered what Tut had told us about positioning the patient on the edge of the bed, with blankets across hips and shoulders; and I put the prepared tray on her locker and got ready.

"You can do the puncture, Blunt," Dr. Clifford said. "I'll hold the test tube for you, and nurse can look after Miss Harris."

Buster went along to the basin by the annex door and scrubbed up. Dr. Clifford took the dressing towel by its corners and spread it on the edge of the bed, over the little rubber sheet I'd remembered to tuck under Miss Harris's hips.

She was trembling. "What do they do this for?" she asked me. "Last time I had it, it left me with a terrible headache."

"It's to—to collect a specimen of your cerebrospinal fluid." I told her. "The fluid that's in your spine, as it were." I added brightly, "The doctor wants to examine it microscopically."

Dr. Clifford grunted. "We're only going to draw off a little fluid, Miss Harris. Principally I want to see whether it's under pressure or not. It may explain some of the symptoms you've been having, you see. And don't worry about having a headache afterward—that's caused by the lowering of pressure, but we shall replace the fluid we take away with a saline solution, so it won't happen this time." He looked at me. "Have you saline ready, nurse?"

I released Miss Harris's knees and neck and flew out into the bathroom. Staff was sitting on a chair, trying to swallow a Ryle's tube. "Saline," I said. "For a lumbar puncture. Does it have to be hot or cold or what?"

Marshall stared at me. "A lumbar puncture? Body temp, of course. Haven't you finished those trolley books yet?"

"Not for the books," I explained hastily. "Dr. Clifford. He's doing one on Miss Harris."

Staff dragged out the tube and gulped. "He doing one—my hat, let me get out there. Where's my cap?" She shot over to the mirror and began to tidy herself.

"It's all right," I told her. "Everything's under control. I only want the saline. He's got the tray and everything and—"

"What tray?" She looked at me sharply. "What tray, nurse?"

"Why, the one you set, of course. It was a dispensation of—"

She pushed me on one side and raced into the ward. I looked at Marshall in bewilderment. "Now what have I done?"

"It's what you *haven't* done, dear girl!" She sighed. "You ass—that tray wasn't sterile! Tinsley only did it to show you—not a thing on it had been boiled."

I gasped. "Oh, Lord! I never thought. What if he's used it?"

"What indeed! You'd better go and see, hadn't you?"

Dr. Clifford was stalking away up the ward with his head in the air, and Buster was scuttering along behind him. "I'm sorry," he said coldly. "I really can't wait any longer, Nurse Tinsley. Call my houseman when the tray is ready, please. As quickly as possible."

The doors flapped together behind them, and Staff came from behind the screens with her face scarlet.

"You fathead!" she said as she passed me. "How could you?" She stopped and turned around as she reached the annex doors. "You'd better get on with the teas—at least you can't go wrong with those, I should hope."

I could have kicked myself.

When we went over for our own tea Noble said, "Cheer up, chick! She won't tell sister, you know. Lots would—but not Staff Tinsley. She isn't that kind."

"Won't she?" I said drearily. "I don't care if she does. That isn't what's worrying me."

"Then what is? Buster thought it was rather funny."

I said that I wasn't bothered about what Buster thought, either. "Don't you see," I said. "It's Dr. Clifford—he thinks I'm just an incompetent fool."

Noble flung open the dining-room door and urged me inside. "More fool him," she commented, "for expecting a new probationer to know all the answers. If he thinks anything about it at all, he can only blame himself."

"But it was my fault," I persisted. "I haven't any excuse. I knew the things had to be sterile—only I was in a fuss."

"Quiet! Look, fruit cake today. Forget the ward for twenty minutes, do!" Noble said. "You have to learn to take these things in your stride, girl. Grow up, can't you?"

But all through tea I was worrying about it. Supposing, I thought, they had actually used the unsterile things and Miss Harris had contracted meningitis or something? Supposing David Clifford had been blamed?

Noble looked at me sidelong as we finished our second cups. "Still brooding, Elliot? What are you doing tonight? It's your evening off. At least you've got that to look forward to. Think of me, on all evening with 'the gorgon,' and count your blessings.''

I stared at her. "My evening? I'd forgotten all about it.'' I had forgotten all about Nigel Enderby, too. Suddenly I began to look forward intensely to his telephone call. He, at least, was not going to know I had made a fool of myself. "I'm staying in,'' I said. "I'm expecting a phone call. I may go out later, I don't know.''

"You do that thing,'' Noble advised me. "What you need—a change of scene.''

She was right. When Nigel phones, I shall go out for an hour or two.

March 19

IT WAS about eight o'clock when the corridor maid came and told me I was wanted on the home telephone.

"Will you take it in the hall booth?'' she said. "It's through to there. It's a gentleman.''

I combed my hair before I went down, and then laughed at myself in the mirror. Nigel was not going to be able to see it. I ran down the stairs to the hall and shut the door after me. "Nurse Elliot speaking,'' I said. "Who is that?''

"Hello, Lucy! It's father. Reporting back.''

"Father! When did you arrive?'' I laughed out of a sense of anticlimax. "I didn't think it would be you.''

"Oh? So many calls from men friends?''

"Silly! Of course not—but I thought you were still in Liverpool. Have you just arrived?''

"About half an hour ago. It—it seems a bit empty without you. I wondered whether you could come over—but I suppose you can't?''

I looked at my watch. "Yes, I can. I'll only have

about an hour and a half with you, though. Unless you can fetch me and bring me back."

"That's just the trouble. I can't. I had to leave the car in town—blew a core plug in Aston and had to go to the nearest garage."

"Bad luck! Look, if I come now I can catch a bus and be with you by a quarter to nine. All right?"

"Fine. I'll have the kettle boiling." He hung up.

I stood there for a moment, wondering what to do about Nigel. I couldn't let father down—but on the other hand I didn't want to miss Nigel. Then I pulled his letter out of my pocket and checked the telephone number. I dialed WYL 5468 and listened to the ringing at the other end.

He answered it himself. "Lucy!" he said delightedly. "I've just been trying to get you but the line was engaged, they said, over to the home. I was hanging around waiting to call again. How are you?"

"Broody," I admitted. "Ward 2 complex mostly." And then I told him I was on my way to see father and explained where his apartment was. "Not far from you," I said. "Would you like to drop in for coffee or something? About half-past nine?"

"Just try me! Love to, if I may. How are you getting back to the grind afterward? Is your father taking you?"

I said I was going by bus, as far as I knew. "So I'll have to leave by a quarter to ten at the latest," I went on. "I have to be in a half-past ten."

"If you go by car you needn't leave until about ten-past ten," he calculated. "That's if you'll risk your life in my rattletrap? Yes?"

I said shamelessly that that was exactly what I had been fishing for.

He was good-natured about it. "I see. Not for the sake of my bright eyes at all, but just to have longer with your parent? The nerve of these modern girls! All right, Lucy. I'll play ball. It'll be a pleasure. See you."

He came around to the apartment at exactly half-past nine, and I had still not explained about him to father. When I let him in at the door I said, "Oh, father, this is Nigel Enderby—he was a patient of ours. He's offered to drive me back, and—"

Father jumped up and held out his hand. "Well, I'm blowed! So we meet again? Sorry we did your people out of the Liverpool job. Better luck next time." He pumped Nigel's hand enthusiastically and pushed him into a chair. "Didn't realize my girl had been hob-nobbing with the opposite camp!"

Nigel's auburn eyebrows shot up in two points. "I'd no idea, sir!" He turned to me. "Wretched girl! You didn't tell me your name was Verney Elliot! This must be a plot."

I sat on the arm of father's chair and blinked. "I'm not with you two at all," I complained. "Opposite camp? Liverpool job? Explain, somebody."

Nigel grinned. "Didn't you know I was with Brindin, Gooch, Marley and Enderby? I'm the Enderby."

I didn't even know that there was an Enderby. I've always known father's biggest rivals as Brindin, Gooch and Marley. He has often told me about them, and how they have been in competition for some of his biggest jobs. "I had no idea you were an architect," I confessed. "I imagined you as a—dental student or something. That's nice."

"Not so nice, Lucy," father smiled. "It was this young man's design that beat mine in the People's Theatre competition."

I remember how disappointed he was over that—he had been pretty sure of the work on that. "Then it must have been outstandingly good," I said loyally.

"It was," Nigel informed me. "I aim to be good."

He looked at father. "I didn't have a shot at the Liverpool one—so I'm glad you collared it. But I'm certainly thinking about St. Timothy's Outpatient Department, so I give you fair warning, sir!"

I went out and fetched the coffee tray in and left them talking shop.

They talked shop solidly until it was time for me to go back. When Nigel was out in the hall finding our coats, father said, "That's an up-and-coming young fellow, Lucy. Wouldn't mind having him in the—in the firm."

"I thought you were going to say, 'in the family,' father," I said. "I've only known him a week or so! Patience, please! I've a career to think of."

"Well," father smiled. "I wouldn't mind that, either. Who do you think will carry on when I'm finished? Lines is on his last legs now—and I don't want Verney Elliot and Lines to disintegrate altogether."

"It won't," I said. "You'll find a younger partner, I expect."

"Quite." He took my coat from Nigel and put it around my shoulders. "That's what I meant." When he saw us out he said, "Glad to see you here any time, Enderby. Not far for you to come is it? Can't get a word in edgeways with this girl of mine here."

"I know, sir. Ghastly, isn't it? She's just the same in hospital—prattling away, forgetting to rub chaps' backs and so forth. Not her fault I came out of it alive, I can tell you!" They shook hands, and father waved us off.

Five minutes away from the home, in a quiet side road, Nigel stopped the car and slid one arm along my shoulders. "Lucy. So nice to see you again." He switched off the panel lights on the dashboard and pulled me closer.

"Nice to see you," I told him. "I needed a lift. I've nearly run away once or twice this week. You're just what the doctor ordered: somebody cheerful." I turned my head to look at him, and his eyes were very bright and very close to mine. "Let's—let's get back, shall we? I've only five minutes to beat the clock."

He leaned over and kissed the end of my nose quickly. "Sure. You're sweet, Lucy." Then he started the engine and drove around to the Home at full speed.

Outside the front door there was a little scurry of latecomers hurrying in, and Braich-Jones was among them. She saw me getting out of the car and waited for me in the hall. "Wasn't that young Enderby?"

"It was," I admitted. "Any objection?"

"Not from me," she said. "But if I'd been keen, I might have felt you had a unfair advantage. We got on very nicely until he found out who you were!"

"What do you mean? Who *I* was?" I fell into step with her to climb the stairs. "I don't follow."

"Well, perhaps I should say when he found out who your father was. It was after that he asked me to bring you that note. Up till then he hadn't seemed so interested, I must say."

My heart sank. So Nigel had not wanted to see me for myself after all, but just because father was Robert Verney Elliot. And then in self-defense, my disappointment gave way to sheer temper. It was a childish reaction, I know, but it has been quite a week, one way and another. I pulled Braich-Jones into my room and slapped the box of nylons into her palm. "There," I said. "That ought to last you quite a time. They're not my size. Not nearly big enough." And then I went to bed and cried.

March 21

THIS IS THE DAY we have all been waiting for, at last. The day of the change. The lists are too long for night sister to read, and they are pinned up in the hall instead. We had to fight our way through the crowd at coffee time to find out where we should be going after lunch at two o'clock.

Everybody moves at this time, even most of the staff nurses, and only the ward sisters and ward maids stay put, except for just a few people who have moved during the last day or two.

I was afraid I might have to remain on Ward 2, with "the gorgon," as I've not been there long. But when I finally found my name on the long list, I sighed with relief. I am back in the children's ward again with Sister Hawthorn, and that is the best news I've had for ages.

But Staff Dodman has her ward sister's blues at last, and she is now in charge of Ward 4. Staff Haarstein had come to the children's from Ward 7—she is the only nurse I know. Our third year is an Indian girl, named Shunala, and the second year is a thirty-year-old ex-typist named Heddle-White, who wants to be a medical missionary and has strange light blue eyes full of fanatic zeal. The other junior is a frightened little thing who has come here from Ward 8, where she seems to have nearly had a nervous breakdown. When we arrived in the ward Sister Hawthorn told me, "Now, you've been here before, nurse. You must show Nurse Tealbury where things are kept and what I like done." She gave me a secret smile and added, "She has not been very happy, so far. You must try to cheer her up."

I said I would do my best and dragged Tealbury out into the annex to show her around. "I remember you," she told me. I looked at her thin face and pink-rimmed eyes and the babyish straggle of silvery hair, and tried to place her. "I was leaving the P.T.S. as you arrived."

"That's right," I agreed. "That makes you six weeks senior to me, doesn't it? So you're pro 3 and I'm pro 4, on the ward." I consulted the routine lists on the bathroom wall. "That takes you for the bathroom and mattress room and me for the sluice room as usual. What I'd give to have something different to look after! How splendid to be a third year and only tidy the linen room."

"I'll do the sluice room if you like," she offered. "I don't mind, honestly. After all, what's six weeks?"

"According to Greta Braich-Jones," I said, "even six days' seniority is enough to make some people put on side. But I've a better idea still. Why don't we do all our jobs together? Teamwork, you know. It might be quicker."

"What will sister say, though?"

"She won't know. And I don't suppose she'd mind— the thing is to get the things done." I looked at the list again. "According to this, you should be blanket bathing five patients, and I should be cutting bread and butter. So we'll do the baths together, and then I'll cut and you can spread."

But in the middle of the first bath, sister called me. "It's nice of you to help Nurse Tealbury," she said, "but I wish you'd do the bread and butter first, nurse. Because I may want you to take a case to the operating room."

"Oh, sister! But I've never—"

"I know, nurse. We all have to go for the first time sooner or later. And it will be much easier to take a child than to take an adult, won't it? The R.S.O. is going to do that pyloric of ours, if he can fit it in—in the first cubicle." I looked through the glass wall at the wizened baby in the first cot. He looked like a little old man. "He's been prepared, and you'll have to hold his legs on the table, because he'll only have a local. So get your teas ahead, in case."

I swallowed and said, "Yes, sister. Very well, sister," and bolted into the kitchen.

I had just finished the stack of bread slices when the telephone rang, and I went out to answer it, but sister was there ahead of me. I would have liked to see Sister Heywood-Bence answer a telephone while there was anyone else to do it. She said, "Yes, yes. I see. Very well. Straight away." Then she came out to me and nodded.

"Yes, nurse. It's the operating room for you. Now, listen to what you have to do. Take the baby in a white blanket—you'll find he's already encased in a cotton-wool and Gamgee-tissue boiler suit to keep him warm. Just see that his diaper is dry before you wrap him up. Wait in the anesthetic room until they call you, then go straight through into the operating room and put him on the table. Sister will show you what to do after that. You won't have to do anything for the anesthetist, this time, at all. Is that clear?"

"Yes, sister." And then I asked, "Just what do they do? And how long will it take?"

"It will be very quick indeed, nurse. All they have to do is first inject an anesthetic, then open up a small incision—in the median line, usually, so that they can get at the pylorus muscle. Then a slit in the muscle, and that's all. Then they stitch up. Now—after they've stitched up, they put on a pyloric corset, as we call it; a little corset made of wide strapping and laced together with tape, to keep his tummy controlled. We send them up from the ward. Here it is. Put it with a spare diaper and give it to sister when you have taken him in."

I took the roll from her and nodded. "Yes, sister. Sister—is there anything at all that I might do wrong?"

She considered, smiling. "I hardly think so, nurse. So long as you keep your hands out of sight, under the blankets, you can't go wrong."

I rolled the little mite in his blanket, hanging ready on the foot of the bed and took him out into the corridor. Sister said, "Use the elevator, nurse, and cross to the block on the ground floor. Don't go across the bridge." I wondered, from the expression on her face, whether she imagined that I didn't know the difference between a baby and a glove drum, but I didn't dare to smile because I was trembling so much that I had to keep my teeth clamped together.

The anesthic room was empty, and I leaned on the blanketed trolley and waited. The baby was pretty doped, but every now and then he gave a feeble kitten-like whimper and burrowed his head into the blanket, gnawing frantically at his fingers. After a while the theater pro came out with a gallipot in her hand. "Here's some glycerine and honey," she said. "Let him nibble your finger dipped in that, if he cries on the table." I suppose I must have looked pretty blank, because she added, "To keep his abdominal muscles from tensing up. Got it?"

"Yes," I agreed. "Only sister told me I'd have to hold his legs."

"Oh, dear. Do you mean to say she's only sent one of you? She knows we need two, for a py. Isn't there anyone else to spare?"

I shook my head. "There's only the other junior on," I said. "And she'll have the teas to cope with. Staff and the other two have gone off."

She sighed noisily. "Confound her. That means I shall have to take one end. All right—you take his legs, then, and I'll take his head. And bring this gallipot in with you when you come. I'll tell you when."

It seemed a long time before she held the door open and said, "Right, nurse. Ready for the pyloric baby."

I remembered the corset. Sister was standing behind a trolley full of instruments, and I held it out to her and said, "Sister said I was to give you this, sister."

There was a muffled giggle from the pro behind me, and sister's eyes were like fires over her white mask. "Stand back!" she said sharply. "You can see I'm scrubbed up! And where's your own?"

I could have killed the pro. She knew better than I did that I ought to have put on a green sterile gown while I was in the anesthetic room—but she hadn't offered to hold the baby while I did so, or reminded me. Tut had taught us all these things, but they are so easy to forget in the heat of battle, as it were. I also knew perfectly well— with my mind—that sister was clean and that I mustn't touch her or hand her anything unsterile.

I dumped the baby on the table and looked wildly around for someone to hold him. The pro deliberately turned her back and opened a drum behind sister. And then two people rescued me. Greta Braich-Jones—I knew the family eyes—came out of the sterilizing room, and at the same moment I realized that the young man fiddling with syringes at the head of the table was Buster Blunt. Each put out a hand, and I muttered something and flew back for a gown and mask, while they steadied the blanketed morsel that was Baby Black.

When I returned Braich-Jones's big sister whispered to me to hold the baby's legs under the blanket, and brought me a stool to sit on and slipped a sandbag under my arms for leverage. At the top of the table Buster winked, and the operating-room pro, also on a stool, hung onto the baby's shoulders and dipped one finger in the gallipot of glycerine and honey.

The R.S.O., very broad and tall, stood with his gloved hands high and looked at sister. "Right?"

She nodded. The man facing Dr. Broadhurst—I could not recognize his eyes or his shape—took the large syringe and began to inject into the creased, dry, lifeless skin of the baby's abdomen. He put the needle in four times, to make a diamond-shaped block of numbness, and then he took the swab sister passed him and painted the skin with yellow lotion. I suppose it must have been picric acid or something of the sort. The baby's legs jerked, and I steadied them, with his tiny ankles like a bird's between my fingers. I was afraid they would snap.

The R.S.O. held out his hand, and sister slapped a scalpel into the palm. Very gently he made his incision—

no more than a thin, red, pencil line across the yellow skin. He barely seemed to stroke the surface. And then it was no time at all before he had hooked out the pylorus, snicked the muscle through and pushed it into place again. I felt very hot in the humid atmosphere of the operating room and my eyes pricked. I realized it had to be hot to save the baby from shock, but it was like a greenhouse—like the palm house at the Botanical Gardens, I remember thinking.

And then somebody was pinching the back of my neck. "Brace up!" hissed Greta Braich-Jones. "Nearly done." She wiped my face with a cold, wet swab, and I blinked and took a fresh hold on the tiny feet. They were fixing the corset over a gauze dressing, and sister had taken off her gloves and was helping Buster to fasten it. The R.S.O. and his assistant were walking across to the sinks to wash. I must have been out for a minute or two, but nobody except Braich-Jones senior seemed to have noticed anything.

It was not until I got down from the stool and tried to straighten my stiffened arms and legs that I looked at the clock. We had only been in the operating room twelve minutes. Yet it seemed an hour. Sister said, "Are you all right, ward nurse?"

I said I thought I was and gripped the edge of the table.

She looked at me quickly. "You'd better let Nurse Witherspoon take the child back," she told me. "You unfasten your collar and get a drink of water from the anesthetic-room tap. Run along!"

I didn't exactly run. I don't think I could even have walked, if it hadn't been for the arm that went around me halfway across the operating-room corridor. I said, "Thanks, Dr. Blunt," and leaned on him heavily, then took the glass of water.

When I had drunk half of the beautiful frosty stuff, I put the glass down and said, "Phew...was it hot in there! Well, at least I didn't pass out on the operating-room floor in the middle of the operation.''

"No, you certainly didn't. You did very well, for a first visit.'' It was not Buster. It was Dr. Clifford. And he still had an arm around my waist.

I stared and tried to collect myself. "I'm—I'm sorry,'' I said. "I had no idea it was you, sir. I thought it was Dr. Blunt. You—you weren't in the operating room, were you?'' I moved self-consciously away from his hand.

"No. I came in at the end looking for my H.P., that's all; and the first thing I saw was Nurse Elliot weaving about all over the place.''

I felt for my mask and found it dangling under my chin, where he had pulled it to give me the water. "How—how did you recognize me, sir, in a mask?''

He smiled down at me. "Your turban isn't very well secured, is it? There's no mistaking your hair. Nobody else in the hospital wears it so short—or has hair as black.'' He put up his hand and gently pushed back the straggles of my damp cockscomb, still dewy from Braich-Jones's wet swab. "Pictish stock, I'd guess.''

His touch did things to my insides that nothing had ever done before. I wanted to put my own fingers over his, but I wouldn't have had the nerve.

"Lowland Scot,'' I said. "If that's Pictish?'' And then I wriggled out of the green gown and reached for my own cap from the hook on the wall.

"Could be.'' He straightened up. "All right now?''

I went down to the ward walking on clouds of lambs-wool and not in the least aware of anything or anybody I passed on the way. The baby was there first, and sister was tucking him up. She looked at me when I walked in. I said, "I'm awfully sorry, sister. I felt a bit queasy, and sister sent me for a drink. That's why I'm late.''

"You've done well, nurse. I half expected you to be

sent out after the first five minutes! You won't mind next time, will you?''

I shook my head. "No, I shall never mind again, sister. Is—is the baby all right?''

"He's fine. Look at him." She nodded down at the screwed up little face. "You see how dehydrated he is now? Look again in about three days' time, and you'll be surprised. We're going to feed him on buttermilk now—that's Dr. Clifford's pet recipe for these weak babies—and he'll soon gain all the weight he lost in the first few weeks. It's one of the most dramatic changes you are ever likely to see in such a young child, barring tracheotomy, of course.''

I looked at his charts. He was just six weeks old. "He's so tiny," I said. "You'd think it would kill him.''

"No. There's very little shock with a local anesthetic and a quick operation. Now he will have some blood into the fontanel, and then he'll be fine.''

"Into the fortanel?" I touched the bulging membranes under the thin skin of his scalp. "Why there, sister?''

She turned his tiny wrist, and pushed back the Gamgee tissue that cuddled it and showed me the inner side of his stick of an arm. "Would you like to try to get a transfusion into veins that size, nurse? Hardly! We wouldn't be able to find a needle small enough, let alone a cannula. And if we did, the blood wouldn't be able to run freely. So we put it into his head instead. It absorbs well from there.''

"I see, sister, Thank you, sister." Then I thought of something else, though I knew I ought to be helping Tealbury with the teas. "Sister—do I get a tick on my chart for going to the operating room?''

"Yes, nurse, I think so. You didn't disgrace yourself! Remind me, before you go off duty, will you?''

Sister Hawthorn is a very nice woman. In fact, hers is a very pleasant ward to be on, and I'm glad I'm back.

March 24

SISTER HAS MADE OUT a new off-duty sheet, and she says that our days and half days will be permanently fixed now, unless we want to change for personal reasons, when she will do her best for us. How different from Ward 2, where duty times are changed at a moment's notice! So this week I am to have an evening today and my day off tomorrow. This means that I can sleep out, if I like, or I can have breakfast in bed tomorrow by putting my name on the list in the dining room. And next week I shall have a half day on Thursday and on Sunday, too.

I know my bedroom isn't yet ready for me at the apartment, but I am going home nevertheless because it will be the first time I have slept away from hospital for seventy-three nights, and it will be wonderful not to be wakened by the sound of night nurse banging open the doors and shouting, "Six o'clock, nurse!" as each one crashes back on the iron of the bedstead behind it, and the light snaps on. It will also be wonderful not to have to put out my light at half-past ten, and (frankly) not to have Braich-Jones wandering in to borrow something or just to see what I am doing.

Peta wrote to me today to say she was being sent to our convalescent home at Broth shortly, and she wants to see me before she goes. She has still not properly answered my letter to commiserate with her about her kidney troubles. Maybe that's what she wants to talk about. If they will let me see her tomorrow, I shall go there in the afternoon. She says she has had "a huge bouquet of carnations and a get-well card from Mr. Hyde." I never thought Mr. Hyde had it in him. Evidently he has still not managed to get another clerk for the bank. I don't believe he is the kind of man who ever does anything without an eye to the main chance, but I shan't tell Peta so.

I have just remembered that I forgot to tell father what Miss Petrie said about knowing someone who wants The Laurels. I must tell him tonight as soon as I get home. He will also be very surprised to hear that I have had my first trip to the theater.

I know it's all wrong of me, but I still keep thinking of David Clifford's fingers touching my hair. It was such a strange sensation, as though, if it had been dark in the anesthetic room, anyone standing nearby could have seen faint blue sparks leaping the gap between his hand and my untidy cockscomb. I know that this is not just a wild theory because I have seen it happen often when I have stroked a cat in the dark, and George Cansdale once did a television program about cats and explained that that is why they don't like being rubbed the wrong way—the tiny sparks irritate their skins and their sensitive whiskers.

It didn't irritate me. It was the most blessed, calming thing I have ever experienced. Maybe it is true that some people do have a "healing touch." Father says mother had it. If there is such a thing, I'm sure David Clifford has it. I suppose that's why he is such a good doctor. Staff Haarstein has it, too, I think. When she picks up a baby it sighs and relaxes at once, even if it has been bawling its head off a moment before.

Maybe I shall be able to cultivate it one day, though I think it must be something people like them are born with. I know that if I had the world's worst headache I should only have to ask Dr. Clifford to lay on his hands, and it would melt away like mist before the sun. How Braich-Jones would laugh, if she were to read that!

CHAPTER FIVE

March 25

FATHER WASN'T expecting me when I walked in last night, and his face lighted up as I opened the door. He was sitting by the fire with papers scattered all over the hearthrug, and he jumped up to hug me.

"Lucy! I wasn't expecting you so soon! What time have you to go back?" He picked up his jacket and struggled into it. "Have you had a meal? Are you hungry?"

I pushed him back into the big armchair and sat on the arm beside him. "I haven't to be back until tomorrow night. Isn't it heaven? And I'm not in the least hungry—but if you are I'll cook you something this minute." I stroked his graying hair back. "Have I interrupted something?"

"Not a bit." He kneeled down to gather the scattered sheets. "I was just doodling. I've had the details of the extensions at St. Timothy's today, by the way. Hope you don't mind if I have a go?"

I got down to help him. "Mind? I shall be wild if you don't land the job! I'm banking on being 'daughter to the architect'; it'll be my only chance of fame."

"Hmm!" Father stood up and looked at me pityingly. "You don't think one person in a hundred cares who designed the place, do you? They ask, 'Who built it?' 'How much did it cost?' and all the rest of it—but do they ever ask who planned it? Not likely! Not until something goes wrong—then it's 'badly designed.'"

"That's life," I said. "But I hope you get it, all the same. You can't let Nigel Enderby beat you this time."

He stacked his papers thoughtfully on the table. "No. I suppose not. But you must be feeling a little divided loyalty?"

I told him just how divided my loyalty was not. I don't think he believed me.

Over tea and sandwiches, later, I said, "Oh! I nearly forgot. Miss Petrie says she knows somebody who's interested in The Laurels. I meant to tell you before, but it went out of my head. Fact is, I don't want anyone else to have the house, I think. I hate to think of it being turned into offices or having people in it who don't care about it."

Father put down his cup and didn't meet my eyes. "As a matter of fact, I've been putting off telling you, too. Lucy—it's sold. Sorry."

I swallowed half a sandwich and nearly choked. "No! When? To people—or to a firm?" I frowned. "I just hate the idea." I imagined the old house being turned into badly proportioned apartments or having its front windows lined with wire gauze and nameplates. "Tell me the worst."

"It's not the worst. It's gone to a private buyer—it'll be run as a private house. And I can't tell you who it is because I simply don't know myself yet. I only know that it's a client of Purdom and Appleby's. Their managing clerk completed the deal with me. And I got my price—four thousand five hundred."

"I'm glad about that, anyway. It's no longer a fashionable district, is it? But at least it's peaceful and away from the noisy areas, and that's a lot nowdays." I felt near to tears—I was born at The Laurels, and it's like losing a bit of myself. I know every corner of the garden and every chip off the paint in the house.

"Your mother never liked it, you know. Said it gave her the creeps. I suppose we would have moved, if—"

"I never knew that she didn't like it." I said. "I feel better about it, if that's so."

Father smiled ruefully. "That's so. She'd have liked to be out among the fields, in the wilds. And she always longed for the hills. I suppose she missed them—after being born under Froggatt Edge, but we had no time."

I got up quickly. "I know it's early, father, but I think I'll go to bed. I've found the blankets and stuff—do you mind if I desert you?"

He said he would soon be off himself, and I kissed him and said good-night. "Don't tidy up," I told him. "I'll have all the time in the world tomorrow. I shall enjoy it."

I had been in bed about ten minutes when I heard the telephone ring. I listened to father pottering along the passage outside my room to answer it. "Yes," he said. "Yes, of course, old chap. No—she's here, as a matter of fact. Half a minute."

I closed my eyes until he had latched my door again.

"Seems to be asleep," he said. "Yes, by all means. Why not call around in the morning—she's sure to be in then, doing the chores, you know. I'll tell her. About eleven, yes. Good night, Enderby."

So it *was* Nigel. I closed my eyes again then and went to sleep. I had only wanted to be sure that it wasn't the hospital. Not that that was likely. I was not yet at the stage where I would be mobilized in an emergency.

March 25 continued

FATHER WILL NOT be home at his usual teatime, and I have been here at The Laurels since shortly before eleven. I had to take one last look, now that I know it's sold at last. I have been sitting on the floor in my old room and remembering so many things. There is still the mark on the wallpaper that always looked like a witch's face, and the window still looks slightly lopsided without curtains. Outside, the garden is a jungle, but my old swing is caught up into its hook on the apple bough, and the hideaway I built beyond the raspberry canes still shows its dark tunnel entrance against the wall where the peach tree used to grow.

In the dining room I found a couple of old chessmen; in the kitchen is last year's calendar, hanging askew from the nail where I used to keep the garage keys. It is all very depressing and nostalgic, and I don't know why I came, except to get away from Nigel.

Even that seems idiotic. Father thought so. At breakfast he announced, "Oh, Nigel Enderby phoned last night, Lucy. Wanted to come around. You'd gone to bed; so I said he might as well call in this morning. All right with you?"

I didn't answer until I had drunk some more tea and refilled both our cups. "I—I don't much want to see him, father. Not today, anyhow. I thought I'd go—go out for awhile."

He raised his eyebrows. "Oh? Sorry, love. Thought you'd be pleased to see him. Well, you needn't answer the door—he knew I hadn't consulted you; so you could easily have made other arrangements. But he's a clever young fellow, you know. I should have thought he was your kind. Good-tempered, too."

"Yes," I nodded, "I know. It's just that I don't want to see him today. That's all. Some other time maybe."

Father got up and reached for his briefcase. "Just as you like, of course. You won't be lonely?"

"Not a bit." I wanted to tell him that I planned to come back here, but I was so afraid that he might tell Nigel. A fine thing, I thought, to have come to the point where I hid things from father. "There are a lot of

hings I want to do. As well as seeing that there's a meal
or you when you come home.''

"You'll put Mrs. Pinson's nose out of joint, you
know. She likes to think she does for me unaided!''

"I'll let her do what she wants, father. I won't interfere at all. But she can clear off early and leave me to
cook your dinner, surely?''

"Better still—she can clear off early, and we'll go out
to dinner. How about that? Like to come up to Birmingham and meet me somewhere?''

"Yes, I'd like to. Where shall we go?''

"Well—are you after good food or glamour?''

I laughed. "I'm a nurse, remember? Food, of
course!''

"Right. Then we'll meet at the St. James's—you
know where it is.''

"New Street? All right, I'll be there. About what
time? Seven?''

He said that would be lovely because he wanted to see
the city surveyor after leaving the office, and he could
do that before meeting me. "He's always on tap until
sixish or after; so I'll come on there when I've see him.
You go on in and wait downstairs in the lounge. None
of your hanging about in the cold—it's an east wind
today.''

I stood at the door and watched him drive away in the
old black sedan that he had had ever since he bought it
new in 1937. One day it will just sit down in the road
and give up the ghost, but until it does I know he will
never bring himself to part with it. Yet he was so different about The Laurels. Maybe mother was fond of
the car—that must be it. She could only have known it
as a new one—because she died when I was two.

It is very cold, sitting here, but I can't bring myself to
say goodbye and leave. I slept in this room for nineteen
years and kept most of my belongings here; I covered

the walls with pinup photographs of Sir Malcolm Sargent and Gregory Peck, Flora Robson, Dr. Schweitzer and Pat Smythe, higgledy-piggledy. And now my new room at the apartment is clean and bare and waiting for me to leave my mark on it. There is not one photograph on the fresh Wedgwood-blue walls and not a chip on the white paint. I would like one picture, but I don't know of what. Something that would lure my eyes away into the distance, like a Russian painting I saw once by a man named Guermacheff or something like that. It was just a sunset pathway between silver birches, and it said everything.

As for pinups—nobody moves me anymore. Nobody but David.

I have been sitting looking at that last sentence for a long time, and it is not cold in this empty room any longer.

But I have no right to write that down or to say it or even to think it. Or even to think of him as David. As far as I am concerned he is Dr. Clifford, consultant physician, who has no coexistence with me at all. I barely touch the fringe of his world; and mine doesn't mean any more to him than if I were a bus driver or a packer in a laundry, or maybe somebody who delivers his morning paper or cleans his shoes. I would be happy to clean his shoes, if it comes to that: they would shine so brightly that the world would know that they had been polished very carefully by somebody who—no. That way madness lies. He is only my grown-up equivalent of Sir Malcolm Sargent, Gregory Peck, Dr. Schweitzer and the rest of them, whose smudgy photographs used to blotch the walls of this room.

I know all this perfectly well with my brain. But I still think of him as David, feel his fingertips in my hair and notice the way his eyes change color, like the sea.

March 28

ON THURSDAY, as I sat daydreaming in my old room at
The Laurels, I heard a car stop outside the house and
then footsteps coming up the flagged path at the front. I
went through to the long landing window, but whoever
it was had passed out of sight, into the porch. And then
the front door creaked open, and somebody was walking through the hall.

Nobody had a key as far as I knew, except the agents,
and maybe the new owner, and I didn't want to meet
either of them, so I stayed very quietly where I was, on
the landing, until I heard the footsteps return to the foot
of the stairs. They hesitated there for a moment, and
then went on, through the front door, and I heard it
echo through the empty house as it closed again.

When I heard the car door slammed, and the note of
the engine drawing away, I went downstairs. Somebody
had left a large packing case in the kitchen, and there
was a round clear patch on the misty window, where
he—or—she had rubbed the glass to look out into the
frost-hazed garden at the back.

At once the house was different. I no longer belonged
to it. It was as alien to me as the packing case and the
swirling marks on the window. I didn't want to stay any
longer. I only wanted to shake off the memory of it and
go.

Mrs. Pinson was busy scrubbing the kitchen floor
when I got back to the apartment. She looked up at me
through a seaweedy straggle of sepia hair, damp with
sweat and grinned. "Guessed you wasn't far away, Miss
Lucy. Why didn't you say? I'd 'ave made you up a bed,
'stead o' you having to do it last night."

"I didn't know I was coming," I said. "Not until the
last moment. Besides—I wanted to surprise father."

She swung out her floor cloth and swooped forward

again with her long red arm. "You want me to get you a bit o' lunch? There's some sausage and bacon I just brought in. An' plenty of eggs. Oh—there was a young chap come. 'Bout eleven o'clock. Now—what was his name?" She sat back on her broad haunches, thinking, with her forehead screwed into tight parallel lines.

"Enderby?" I suggested.

"Ah, that's it. Enderby." Her face cleared, and she bent over the bucket again. "Yes—he seemed to think you'd be in—but I said I knew nothing about it, so he went off again."

"He isn't—he isn't coming back, is he, Mrs. Pinson?"

"Not as I know of, Miss Lucy. No. Said he was off to Birmingham—be at the office, he said, if he was wanted. Perhaps he thought you'd call him?" She stood up slowly and picked up her rubber kneeling mat. "There, that's done. Now I'll get the fire lighted, and you can have a nice sit-down and a cup of coffee, eh?"

"I'll do the coffee," I told her. "You do the fire— I'm no use with fires, I always put them out."

"Unlucky in love then," she opined. "That's what they say, isn't it?" She shoved back the wisps of hair from her face with her big, coarse hand. "Folks who put fires out—they reckon they don't have much luck with their affairs. Says in my little book they 'quench the fires of passion'—what do you know about that?" At the door she paused. "It don't apply the other way, though. I can get a fire going with anybody—but I don't see myself rousing no passionate feelings in anybody!" She laughed comfortably.

I reached for a saucepan from the shelf over the sink. "Go on with you, Mrs. Pinson," I said. "Your husband's very fond of you, anyway! He told me so when he helped us with the moving."

"Go on—he never!" She stared at me. "Honest, Miss

Lucy? My old man said a good word for me? You're kidding!''

"Cross my heart and hope to die," I said. "He said, 'That woman's the apple of my eye, miss.' Truly! He said you were the best cook in England, and that he wouldn't swop you for a couple of film stars.''

Mrs. Pinson's face turned nearly purple with pleasure. "Well! And I never knoo 'e cared! I tell you, you live and learn, don't you?''

"That's right," I agreed. "You certainly do.''

She had a blazing fire going by the time I had made a jug of coffee, and I sat down on a stool in front of it to drink mine and told her all about St. Timothy's while she polished around me.

"I reckon nurses have a 'ard life," she said. "It's not all jam is it? I'd a liked to be a nurse meself, you know. Only I don't reckon I got the book learning for that. Don't bother me, ill folks. But my mother could never touch 'em. Funny, isn't it? Some people, they go all to pieces when there's sickness.''

I told her I thought maybe that was how Peta felt.

"Now I was wondering how Miss Royde was getting on," she said. "Shy, isn't she? Old, like, for her age.''

"Old?" I turned to look at her. "How do you mean, old?''

"Well—" She shifted another yard along the floor with her rags. "Old-fashioned. I always reckoned she'd take up with an older man, you know. Somebody—somebody who'd be like a dad to her, if you get my meaning.''

It was a novel view of Peta—but when I thought it over I saw that Mrs. Pinson had something. Peta had never been at ease with young men. I remembered again about her short-lived affair with the boy in the bank.

"Maybe that's it," I agreed. "She needs someone older.'' And then I thought, maybe I do, too.

We had lunch together at the kitchen table, and Mrs. Pinson told my fortune in the tea leaves afterward. She saw a muddled future, I gathered. "Don't reckon you know what you do want," she warned me. "Or if you do, you don't stand much chance of getting it by the looks of things."

"I know," I said. "Don't tell me. I'm a Capricorn—things never come easily for me. Always the hard way. I'm used to it."

"Ah well," she stacked the cups and saucers and stood up. "More worth having when you get 'em, I expect. Easy come, easy go, you know, miss."

"Yes," I said. "I expect you're right."

I went to sleep in front of the fire after she had gone, and it was dusk when I woke and the fire was sinking. I decided to go up and have a hot bath before I got ready to go into town to meet father. And it was when I was lying soaking, reveling in knowing that nobody was likely to bang at the door and tell me to hurry up, that I remembered I'd left my diary at The Laurels. But where? The last time I had looked at it I had been in my old room, and I had dropped it as I got up to see who was at the door. It must be on the window seat or on the floor nearby.

I hurried into my clothes, locked up and raced around to the old house. There was just time, before catching the bus. I let myself in at the front door—I realized I should have to hand over the key quite soon, but it was still on my key ring and I was glad that it was now—and ran upstairs in the gloom. There was a shaft of light from a street lamp across the road lighting up the room, but I couldn't see the diary anywhere. There was nowhere for it to hide. Maybe I had left it on the landing, I thought. But there I drew a blank, too. And it was not in the kitchen, and I hadn't been anywhere else.

I washed the dust off my hands at the kitchen sink after I had felt all over the floors and ran for the bus at the corner of the road. The diary couldn't have disappeared, surely? And nobody could have taken it—or could someone? And then I realized, with a sigh of relief, that I had had a shopping bag with me, because I had fetched bread on my way, and that the book must be in the bag still. I must have stuffed it in unconsciously.

Father was already waiting for me, and I met him coming up the steps to street level to look for me. "You're late," he said. "Not like you. I thought maybe you'd gone off somewhere with young Enderby and given me the go by!"

I put my hand through his arm, and we rattled down the stairs together. "Not likely! I haven't even seen him." I explained then about going to The Laurels and about losing my diary. "It *must* be in the shopping bag," I said. "Yet I don't remember putting it there. The last time I remember seeing it was up in my old room, near the window."

He patted my arm. "Don't worry. We'll find it. I'll look for it as soon as I get home tonight, and if it isn't in the bag or anywhere around the apartment, I'll go back to The Laurels and have a hunt around. You'd better give me your key, by the way, and I'll let Purdom and Appleby have it. I'd forgotten you still had one."

When we were at the table and he had ordered, I took the key off my ring and watched him put it on his. "Goodbye, Laurels," I said. "Funny—you know, I always took it for granted that there *were* laurels there—but there isn't one, in fact, is there?"

He shook his head. "Not one. There were, mark you. Rows of 'em. But your mother had them rooted out—couldn't stand 'em. Said they depressed her. She planted all that honeysuckle instead, along the wall where the shrubbery used to be. She was quite right—they *are* gloomy plants. But it was considered highly respectable to have them, you know, at one time."

"I know," I said. "Like having an aspidistra in the front window, in one of those ghastly bottle-green pots with the glaze all crackled."

Father grinned. "And plaster Alsatians, and busts of Schubert...."

"And the boy with a thorn in his foot, and presents from Scarborough, and snowstorm paperweights, and—" I stopped.

Father looked up, and then he swiveled around in his chair. "I don't see anything interesting," he complained. "What caught your eye?"

I leaned over to pour him a glass of water. "Nothing," I said. "I thought I saw somebody I knew." And I went on looking at Staff Haarstein's face, lively and lighted with a spark I had never seen in it before, and at the back of the man she was listening to.

Minutes later father kicked me under the table. "Wake up, Lucy! Not hungry?"

"Yes. Sure I'm hungry. Why?"

He nodded at the plate in front of me. "Then dig in, child. Don't let their precious steak get cold—you'll break their hearts. Lots of onions, you note. I remember your fads still, you see."

"Yes." I picked up my fork, and sighed at the size of the steak. "Matron won't let us have onions in hospital. Says the patients don't like the smell. I suppose I oughtn't to eat these, but I shall. Tell me about the new Outpatients Department."

"Well, it'll be about a twenty-thousand job, I think. They want more examination rooms, and the hall enlarged, and another theater, and—"

When he was launched, I didn't even have to listen.

He called me last night. "The diary wasn't in the apartment, Lucy. So I went around to The Laurels this evening and found it."

"Where was it? I couldn't see it anywhere," I said.

"It was on the window seat, in your old room."

"But I *looked*—" It was no use. He would only tell me how evidence can be distorted by the mind. "Thanks so much, father. Where is it now?"

"I'll put it in an envelope and drop it in at the home for you, but it will be very late tonight, after the club dinner. You'll find it in the morning."

I thanked him. And then I said, "Father—don't read it. Please! One day you can—but not yet."

"Just as if! I wouldn't dream of it—you ought to know that, Lucy. When did I ever eavesdrop on your life?"

"Never," I said gratefully. "That's what makes you a unique parent, bless you."

And when home sister gave it to me this morning, this book was wrapped in layer upon layer of paper, each layer sealed with cellulose tape, so that it took me an age to unpack it. It serves me right.

I am so glad to have it back. And I'm still quite sure that it wasn't on the window seat when I went to look for it.

March 31

THIS MORNING I was off from 10:00 until 12:30, and Noble asked me to go with her for a coffee. There is a café not far from the home, and most people go there on short passes, when they are too tired to go farther afield. "The Griddle?" I said. "Well, all right. Suits me. I never see you nowadays."

"You should worry," Noble smiled. "You've got a good selection—who is it, now? Heddle-White—she

gives me the shivers, frankly. And Shunala, and Tealbury. How can you cope?''

''They're all right. Heddle-White is crazy, but she'll
do anything for anybody. She goes out and does the
sluicing for other people to mortify the flesh or something.'' I laughed. ''Very handy.''

''Very. What about the others? Tealbury's a sad one,
isn't she? Always looks as though she'd burst into tears
if anybody said boo to her.''

''She is a bit sniffy,'' I admitted. ''But Sister Fisher
gave her hell up in Ward 8, and she hasn't recovered her
equilibrium yet. She'll be all right when she gets used to
Sister Hawthorn. She's a dear. Shunala's really beautiful, isn't she? And her voice is so soft. You'd never
dream how obstinate she can be, to listen to her. Iron
hand in the velvet glove, you know.''

''All Asiatics are a bit like that,'' Noble admitted. She
pushed open the door of The Griddle and made for the
window table. ''They have a lot of civilized subtlety that
I envy like mad. Imperturbable on top and white hot
underneath. The reverse, in fact, of 'the Gorgon!' '' She
waved the waitress over and asked for coffee and
chocolate biscuits. ''I'm starving!'' she said.

I remembered something then and began to lead up to
it deviously. ''There's Staff Haarstein, of course,'' I
began. ''She's quite a good nurse, and—''

''But so wooden, dear girl! That deadpan expression
strikes a bit chill, doesn't it?''

I thought of Haarstein's lovely pale face as I had seen
it on Thursday evening. ''Oh, she has her moments. Tell
me, Noble—do you remember, once, in Ward 7, saying
something about—about her seeing me with Dr. Clifford? You know, you said she'd think my mind wasn't
on my work.''

Noble frowned, then nodded. ''Yes. I remember.'' She
began to stir her coffee thoughtfully. ''What about it?''

I looked at her hard. "Why did you stall, like that? You were stalling, weren't you?"

"Was I?" She began to unwrap a silver-paper-covered biscuit very carefully. "Now what makes you—" She caught my eye. "All right. Cards on the table. But first—does it matter to you?"

"To me?" I put a lot of effort into opening my eyes very wide. "Why would it? Me, I have an admirer—didn't you know? Nigel Enderby! Sent me some nylons—that shows you."

"Not a very convincing argument—but still—I suppose you mean that you're just curious."

"That's it," I said. "Just plain nosey. Now—what goes?"

"Haarstein and Clifford? I don't know. Not really. But they do spend a lot of time together—everybody knows that." *Everybody but me,* I thought. "And when you come to think of it, they've got a lot in common."

"Yes," I agreed. "Good hands for one thing."

Noble frowned. "Good hands? I hadn't noticed that so much. But they are both rather withdrawn characters, don't you think? Aching heart beneath the smiling face sort of thing. Sounds a bit off the beam automatically speaking, but you know what I mean."

"Yes," I said. "I know what you mean. Introverted."

"Not exactly. Sensitive-with-a-shell, sort of. Autistic, as the trick cyclists say."

"Yes. And you really think there's something in it?"

Noble shrugged. "I wouldn't know. But I'd guess so. She—she lights up when he talks to her. And he does talk to her, even if he is a bit strong and silent with most people."

I changed the subject. "When does the next lot of lectures begin? I suppose you'll take them with my set, won't you?''

"I expect so. Tut only runs one lot for each half year—so that brings me in with your mob because I'm about five months senior to you. It'll be physiology first, before we do any more anatomy. Nice change.''

"Who takes them?''

"No idea. One of the men, I expect. Tut reckons to do anatomy and nursing and hygiene, and then we get various chaps for physiology, medicine and surgery. Last year they had the R.M.O., but since he's still away—''

I realized that I hadn't seen the R.M.O. since he examined me when I applied for admission.

"When does he come back?''

"No idea—he went for three months, didn't he? So he won't be back yet. I don't know what he wants to keep rushing off to these potty conferences for—after all, his job's here, and he isn't doing it.''

"Maybe it's an honor to be sent?''

"To some things, yes. But not this germ warfare thing. It's just morbid. After all—if they want to give us all botulism, what defense is there?''

"Vaccine?'' I suggested. "Immunize everybody?''

Noble snorted. "Yes, like polio. You can shout yourself black in the face at eighty percent of the population before they do anything about it. How do you think they'd be if we were trying to get them vaccinated against Russian germs? They'd laugh. Or they'd say they had conscientious objections.''

"Like Jacqueline's mom,'' I said. "She said she hadn't had her immunization against diphtheria because it went against her conscience. Buster didn't know, and he simply did her, without asking, when Peta Royde went off. That started something, apparently. She wanted him to undo it again!''

"What a hope! What did he say?''

"Nothing, I gather. Sister Hawthorn had a heart-to-heart with her, and she emerged from the linen room a sadder and wiser woman. Or so the story goes. At all events, Braich-Jones told her sister that she brought all the other children up to O.P.D. next day, and asked if they could be done, too. So much for Sister Hawthorn's powers of persuasion." I stood up. "I must go, Noble. I haven't made a clean cap up, and it takes me an age."

She came with me. Along the road I asked her, "What made you give up ballet? Was it a giving up of that or a positive coming to this? I've often wondered."

She smiled. "Do you know, I've often wondered myself. I wasn't a very good dancer—it always seemed to me that there must be something I could do really well. Only I didn't know what. And then I went one day and gave blood at the transfusion center—I suppose I wanted to do something useful, and I am a universal donor. And something got me while I lay there resting. I don't know what. The smell of the place perhaps? I don't know. But it worked in me like a—a ferment, you know. And after I sprained my ankle, I weaned myself off the stage—and here I am. No regrets!"

"None at all?"

She shook her head. "Not one, I promise you. It's a great life. I don't feel half so darned nonproductive as I used to."

I like Noble very much. She is tremendously attractive, too, but she doesn't seem to go about with men friends much. I think she is one of the few people here who is big enough to deliberately put all that on one side for the duration. Except for Heddle-White, of course, and with her it is as much a case of lack of opportunity as of positive renunciation. If Noble can do it, with her looks and charm, I can without them. In any case, I have made up my mind to get state registered—

I'd feel I'd let mother down if I didn't—so what is the use of getting involved with people? I would far rather give something up than have it taken from me—that way I am still in charge. And it ought to be comparatively easy to give up what I have never had and never really stood any chance of having. I don't know why it seems so difficult.

Tut always says, "The way to clarify your thoughts is to write things down on paper."

So here it is. I am going to stop thinking about David and make up my mind to be as good a nurse as I can. It looks quite childish, written down in black and white. But I think I feel less childish than I have ever felt. I won't be twenty until January, but I know what it will feel like to be much older than that, I think. Everything is easier when you feel less horribly young.

April 5

IT WAS NOT until yesterday that I realized that positive action is a lot simpler than negative retreat. The cure was ready in my hand, and I was too stupid to see it. But it came to me during breakfast yesterday, and when I went over for coffee I skimped my bed-making so as to have time for a telephone call.

Brindin, Gooch, Marley and Enderby was a long time answering the telephone, but I got through to Nigel at last. I said, "It's Lucy Elliot...I'm awfully sorry I missed you when you called at the apartment. And that I was out when you phoned the home as well. I don't mean to be elusive." I sounded so arch it made me feel sick, but I pressed on. "I've a free evening tonight—I don't know whether—"

"I'm practically there," he said eagerly. "Dear Lucy! I thought you'd crossed me off your little list."

"I haven't any little list," I said wistfully. "Truly. No

time. And I get so frightfully tired that I can't be bothered to go out; you know how it is?"

"Sure I know. But you'll come out tonight?"

"If—if you'd like me to, Nigel."

"I'll be outside the nurses' home at—what time? Seven?"

"Not outside the home—" I began. And then I thought, why not? Let me be seen with him. It may help. "All right, outside the home," I agreed. "About seven, yes. And if I'm late—you won't go away, will you?"

"If you're late, my sweet, I shall stay there until they put railings around me and people stare at me."

"That," I said, "is not original. It's a direct pinch from Dornford Yates. But never mind. I know what you mean." I hung up—I can't talk at that level for very long. When I saw him, I thought, I would make him understand that all I was offering was my friendship. Just that and no more. He is not important to my career, and so he is not important.

He was outside the front door in his battered little car when I got out just after seven o'clock, and when he saw me he climbed over the top, ran up the home steps to meet me and swung my hands in his. "Nice," he said. "Nice Lucy!"

I frowned. "Please, Mr. Enderby! Let us have a little circumspection. Suppose—suppose Nurse Braich-Jones were to see you!"

Nigel looked at me sharply, and then laughed and helped me into the car. As we drew away from the home he said, "Why Nurse Braich-Jones, of all people?"

"Why not? I gather she had the pleasure of your acquaintance on Ward 7." I wondered why his neck was slowly turning red. "Didn't she?"

"That's one way of putting it. Oh, Lord, Lucy—I'm a man, I'm not supposed to—"

"To what?" I probed. "Kiss and tell?"

The car swerved as he turned to look at me. "Good heavens, no! It wasn't that! Not likely."

"Then what? You may as well tell me," I said. "I'll worm it out of you in the end. I'm very curious now."

He sighed. "Look there's such a thing as—pursuing a chap. Leave it at that."

"I see."

He put out his hand and felt for mine. "You don't see. I simply couldn't tell you—it was ghastly!" He swung the car into the road out of town. "I don't know where we're going—you've embarrassed me until I can't think."

"Tell me," I said. "How did you come to be discussing me with her? Not that I mind or anything. I just wondered how I cropped up."

"Discussing you? Did we?"

"So she says," I told him meanly. "She says you asked questions about me."

"Well, if I did, it was because I wanted to know, I expect. But I don't remember much about it."

I went on relentlessly. "Did you ask her—or did she tell you—who my father was?"

This time Nigel pulled the car into the curb and switched off the engine. He put his arm along the back of the seat and turned to face me. "You know darn well I didn't! What a potty question! If I'd known, would I have been so surprised when I met him?" His face was serious and his eyebrows were down.

"You might—" I said. "Yes, you might."

"That's what you think of me? That I'm a prize liar?" His jaw tightened, and his eyes were steely. "Or are you just indulging in some elaborate leg pulling?" He pulled out a cigarette and lighted it without taking his eyes away.

I nodded. "Good enough Nigel. But I had to ask you,

didn't I? Braich-Jones is a bit apt to distort things, in an accidental-on-purpose sort of way. I just wondered...."

"Then you may as well have it straight. Even if it is unmanly of me. Look—from the second that girl came to the ward she made a dead set for me. It was hell, I can tell you. All the chaps ribbed me about it. That's why I begged to go home so soon. She used to hang around me, gassing, until I could have strangled her. I only mentioned you to her just to give her the general idea that there were other women in my life, so to speak." He flushed. "I may have gushed a fair bit. But your father was never mentioned; that's the truth. I nearly had a fit when I recognized him. It never occurred to me—you see, you don't use the Verney part, do you?"

I shook my head. "No. Father only uses it because there are two other Robert Elliots in the same job; so he signs his plans with the Verney to distinguish them. So he sticks to it for professional purposes. It's easier."

Nigel smiled and turned back to the wheel. "Well, that seems to be that, Lucy. Now—where shall we go?"

"How about Whittington?"

"The golf club, you mean? Ah, that's an idea! If you're a member. I'm not. I've heard tell that it's possible to be reasonably well fed there."

"Reasonably," I said, "is something of an understatement. Robert seems to have an idea that one day somebody will burst, and he means to be there to see it happen! His wife's a cracking cook."

"Right. Whittington—here we come!" The little car surged forward along the Lichfield Road, and I snuggled down into my fur collar and let the cold wind cool my cheeks.

I was nervous as we walked up to the lounge entrance. Nigel sensed it at once. He was more perceptive, I decided, than I'd given him credit for. "What's up?" he said kindly. "Some of your creditors' cars outside or some-thing?"

"No. I just thought—we might meet somebody I know."

"So?"

"So nothing," I said. "Go on in—it's cold out here." I took a deep dreath and marched straight in.

There was somebody I knew—but I needn't have wor-ried. It was Mr. Hyde. He was all alone, playing with the slot machine, and when I'd talked nicely to Robert about a grill I took Nigel over and introduced him to Mr. Hyde.

"Bless my soul!" Mr. Hyde said. "You don't still have time for amusement, do you, Miss Elliot?" He smiled. "I thought nurses spent all their spare time with their shoes off, groaning."

"Now what gave you that idea, Mr. Hyde?" I pro-tested. "It's a lie."

He produced two pink patches on his cheekbones. "As a matter of fact," he confessed, "I had a letter from P—from Miss Royde. She told me. I'm glad she's giving it up, I may say. Seems to have knocked her about a bit."

He looked at Nigel. "You know Miss Royde, Mr. Enderby? No? A very nice young woman. Very nice. Not like some of these modern girls you know. None of this rock 'n' roll mentality; my word, no. Very sensible."

I was startled. When we had been at the bank I hadn't noticed that he thought Peta particularly sensible. Evidently he had begun to appreciate her better qualities since he lost her.

What had Mrs. Pinson said about Peta needing an older man? I began to smile, just thinking about it, and had to hide my face by putting sixpence in the slot machine. For the first time ever I struck the jackpot and sixpences strewed the floor.

"That's lucky," Mr. Hyde said. "I've put eight in, and only won two shillings. It must be your lucky day."

I wonder if he was right. Certainly my viewpoint has changed a good deal since talking to Nigel. It is good to know that Braich-Jones didn't tell me the strict truth— and that he didn't know who father was. Not that I can see what he would have to gain, even if he did, but then I don't understand business tactics and never did.

Nigel is great fun really. He made me laugh a great deal over our meal. And when he took me back to the home I hadn't the heart to make my speech about platonic friendship. I just kissed him good-night when he asked me to, without arguing. It seemed the natural thing to do at the time; and he was very gentle about it.

I'm not weakening. I'm still planning to keep things on a noninvolved plan. But I may as well do it as pleasantly as possible—hair shirts and peas in the shoes are no longer quite the thing. They would only remind me of David—not help me to keep him in his pigeon-hole.

CHAPTER SIX

April 8

IT IS ALREADY a quarter-past ten and I shall soon have to put out my light. But so much has happened today— it has been one of those black and white days, full of contrasts, but they will fade to gray because of being mixed unless I write them down while they are fresh.

Not that I shall ever forget our first physiology lecture this morning. Tut fussed us into the classroom the way mothers fuss their children into strange schools—with a look of, "Don't let me down now, or I'll whip you when I get you home," and a general air of seeking to impress and not being quite with us.

We didn't know why, nor did we know why she had put on a fresh cap on a Thursday—she usually sports them on Mondays, Wednesdays and Fridays—until a quiet knock at the door sent her hurtling from her chaperon's seat by the skeleton cupboard, with a red neck and the whites of her eyes showing. Then we saw the point.

When she had escorted him to the desk and shown him where the chalk is kept, she turned to us important-ly and dared us to flicker an eyelash. "We are *very* fortunate to have Dr. Clifford to talk to us today, nurses. He is a *very* busy person, and I am *very* grateful to him for giving up his time."

"So be *very* attentive, or I'll be *very* cross," Noble

murmured at my side. "Is it her only adjective?" She is rather good at talking prison fashion, without moving her lips.

"Adverb," I corrected her.

I am not so well trained, and Tut glared at me. "Nurse Elliot! I am speaking, if you please!" She rapped on the front desk with her knuckles.

"Sorry, sister." I looked down at my notebook as David's head came up and felt myself turning scarlet.

Noble quivered with amusement.

I didn't hear the rest of what Tut said, and I couldn't look up again until I heard the squeak of chalk on the blackboard. He was drawing a diagram of the heart, quickly and effectively, with light confident strokes. When he turned around he cuddled the chalk between his cupped palms and said, "The heart, ladies, is not the seat of the affection, as you may have been led to believe. On the contrary, it is merely a very powerful muscle."

The front row dutifully tittered, and Tut's shoulders wriggled with motherly shame.

"You have learned anatomy," he said. "Into what is the heart divided? Nurse Noble?"

Noble told him. His glance slid past me to Tealbury.

"You, nurse—the fair one at the back." He smiled apologetically. "I'm sorry—I haven't a plan of your names. Perhaps Sister Tutor will let me have one?" Tut muttered and slapped papers about, and Tealbury stood up.

"Nurse Tealbury, sir." She twisted her apron between her fingers and dithered.

"Quite so. Thank you. Nurse, tell me, what is the function of the heart?"

She hesitated. "To—to—" she made wild peristalic motions with her fingers.

"Pump," I whispered, and her face cleared.

"To pump the blood around the body, sir." She sat down again, and Tut stood up.

"Excuse me, sir. Nurse Elliot, will you please come and sit at the front?" She was quite furious, I could see that. "And you go to the back, Nurse Tealbury. I'm sorry, sir. We shall all be very attentive now." Her small eyes dared me to open my mouth again.

David looked at me for the first time, straight between the eyes. His mouth curved in a gentle smile. "While you are on your feet, nurse, perhaps you will come out here and show me the apex of the heart on the diagram."

When I had done that he relaxed, leaned on his elbows and began to talk about auscultation, and the significance of the apex beat. He showed us an old wooden stethoscope, and then pulled his own binaural out of his pocket and passed it around so that we could listen to one another. I had it last, and it fell to me to hand it back. He said, "Thank you, Nurse Elliot," and gave me the same wonderful smile that I had seen for the first time when he had been talking about "the gorgon." Because of that smile, and because his fingers touched mine as he took the stethoscope, I turned away too quickly and knocked all Tut's lists off her desk, sending them flying across the floor.

After that I didn't take in another thing. Not until Tut tackled me as we filed out. She said I was nothing but a badly behaved schoolgirl; that she was quite sure Dr. Clifford was disgusted with me, and that I had let down the hospital. "What's more," she finished, "if this lecture is not written up any better than the last one I gave you, nurse, I shall send you to the matron. I am *very* disappointed in you!"

It was not until she let me go that I realized he was still just outside the classroom door and had heard every word. "Another of the difficult ones," he murmured as

I passed him. "You can take it." And then he went back into the classroom to speak to Tut.

April 9

THERE WAS no time to finish last night. I managed to get my light out just in time, before home sister did her round. I had to get undressed after she had puttered away again. But the rest of the day is still very clear in my mind and would have been even if I hadn't had Nigel's note this morning to remind me of it.

I half-promised on Monday that I would see him on my half day, but we made no definite arrangement, so I was surprised to find him waiting in the home hall at two o'clock.

"All right, Lucy?" he asked. "You're free, aren't you?"

I pushed the thought of David's smile away from me, hard, and reminded myself of the promise I made to myself. "Yes," I said. "I'm free, Nigel. It's my half day, all right."

He ran his hand through his bright hair and frowned. "I want to talk to you. I'm in a bit of a spot. Maybe you can cheer me up."

He looked genuinely worried. "The idea was," I reminded him gently, "that you should cheer me up. Will you wait while I change? What clothes should I put on?"

"Oh—something warm. You know what my car is like." He smiled briefly and not very convincingly. "Don't be long, will you?"

I wasn't long. I was exactly ten minutes. But when I came downstairs again, he was pacing impatiently up and down by the glass door and flung it open as soon as he saw me.

He didn't talk at all until we turned into Bennett's

Hill, and he pulled up outside his office. "Wait here a minute, Lucy. I've got to fetch something."

When he came back he was carrying a big portfolio of drawings. I frowned. "Work?"

"Uh-huh." He started the car again and turned toward home. "Look, Lucy. You remember I did the stuff for the People's Theatre?"

I nodded. "Yes. Oh, of course! It's supposed to be opened by Princess Alexandra next week, isn't it? I'd forgotten."

"That's the point. Things have gone slightly hay-wire—and it isn't going to be ready."

"No? I thought it was ready." I put my hand on his arm. "Anyway, if it isn't, it's not your fault. It's the contractors', surely?"

He grunted. "It isn't that. Lucy—they waited until now—now—to find out that the acoustics are impossible. God knows where I went wrong. I've gone over and over it, and I can't see where I've slipped up."

"Oh, dear. Well—can't they fit up a—series of baffles or something? I'm sorry, I don't really know the jargon."

"You don't need to."

"Then how can I help?" I looked at the portfolio between us. "I'm no use to you, Nigel."

He looked at me quickly and then back at the road again. "I wouldn't do this if I weren't worried sick," he said. "I—I want you to ask your father to help me. As a favor to you, if you like. Just so that he does." He put his hand on mine. "Will you, Lucy?"

"Of course—if that's what you want. But why can't you talk to your own firm? What are Brindin, Gooch and Marley doing?"

He let out his breath sharply. "I told you I was in a spot. They've washed their hands of the whole thing, because I got the job without letting them in on it in the first place. You see, we only reckon to send in one design from any one firm, and Gooch had an entry— Now they've disowned mine, because it spoiled his chances.''

"I just don't understand it,'' I said. "It sounds awfully childish to me. Or is it a question of ethics? Tut's always talking about professional ethics. Is that it?''

"Yes, more or less. Only more feverish than usual because I'm the new boy.'' His lips tightened.

"We could have gone around to father's office,'' I suggested. "He won't be home until half-past five.''

"Now that would be quite unethical. That would be the last straw—I'd be right out on my ear if I did that. Have a bit of imagination, Lucy, dear! Do doctors take their failures around to one another's consulting rooms?''

"Yes, in hospital they often look at one another's cases,'' I said reasonably. "Why not?''

"Well, they don't as between one GP and another, I can assure you. They call in a specialist or—''

"I see. You're calling in father, as it were?''

"That's it. If you can persuade him. I've got to talk to somebody. Somehow this thing has to be put right before the opening. If it's not, I shall be the laughing stock of the press—and so will the firm. And that will hardly do me any good.''

"No, I suppose not. I'm sure father will help, Nigel. We'll go home and get Mrs. Pinson to give us some tea, and then it won't be long before he comes.''

We drove past The Laurels, and there was new white paint on the window frames. At the apartment, we found Mrs. Pinson had gone, but there was a good fire in the sitting room, and when I'd made some tea we pulled the studio couch up in front of it and sat there with the tray between us.

I had been toasting my toes for several minutes, thinking what a fool I had made of myself at the physiology lecture, when Nigel suddenly picked up the tray, set it carefully on the floor and sat close to me.

I looked up at him inquiringly. "Nigel?"

"Lucy, be kind. I'm so damned fed up, I—" He put both arms around me and dragged me against his shoulder. "Oh, hell!" His mouth burrowed into my neck, and then he tilted up my chin and kissed me on the lips. It was a kiss that went on for a long time, and it was very pleasant. Or it would have been if I had not realized that he felt horribly miserable and was kissing me to reassure himself.

When he took his mouth away, I put my arms around his neck. "It's all right, Nigel. Don't worry. Everything will be all right. You'll see."

We sat there for some time, not saying anything, and we were still there when Mrs. Pinson's key grated in the lock. Nigel stood up and pushed his hair back. "Your father?"

"No, it's Mrs. Pinson with the shopping. Relax. I'll ask her to find us something to eat now."

"No—don't do that. I'm not hungry. Are you?"

I certainly was. I left him while I went out to the kitchen and explained. "And I'm starving," I told her. "Can I make some toast, or are you short of bread? Father wasn't expecting me."

"I'll make it, Miss Lucy," she said. "Don't you fret. You go back to your young man."

"He isn't my young man," I protested. "He's only a friend."

"That's what they all say. You run along, and I'll bring you a tray in, in a minute. Rude, it is, leaving guests!"

I gave up and went back to Nigel. Then he did surprise me. He took me by the elbows, on the hearthrug, and jerked out, "Lucy—I didn't mean to say this yet, but—"

"But what?" I smiled up at him, and said unthinkingly, "Is this a proposal, Mr. Enderby?"

"I'm afraid so, Lucy. Will you?"

I stared. "Will I what?" I swallowed. "You're not asking me—"

"I'm trying to ask you to marry me. Only I'm out of practice." He smiled lopsidedly. "I haven't asked anyone lately, you see."

"But, Nigel—we've only known each other since—"

"Does that matter?" His arms came around me again.

"Darling, what difference does that make? I—I'm horribly in love with you. Do you mind?"

There is a little warning voice somewhere inside my head that always seems to butt in whenever things are getting exciting. Even when I was a child, it spoiled some of my best adventures by chipping in with, "Now, Lucy—be careful!" And it did when Nigel leaned over to kiss me again.

I pushed him away. "No," I said abruptly. "It's crazy." And then Mrs. Pinson came in with the tray, and he made polite conversation with her—because I kept the ball rolling—until father's car turned into the drive.

He didn't mention the People's Theatre until after tea. And then I said, "Father—Nigel's wanting your advice. On a little matter of acoustics."

"Tricky things, accoustics," he said. And he looked across at Nigel. "I suppose I know about it already. You don't keep a thing like that secret, you know. It's all over town. Next thing you know there'll be headlines—"

"Father! Please help Nigel. It's rotten for him, after—"

"Help him? *I* help him?" Father's gray eyes were wide with horror. "But I *can't,* Lucy. It wouldn't be—"

"Ethical!" I burst out. "How can you be so stuffy? I'm asking you as a personal favor. Of course you can be unethical if you want to."

Father shook his head slowly from side to side, and Nigel sighed noisily. "I might stretch a point if he were my son, for example—but even the—"

And then I jumped to it. Because they had both hammed it a bit too hard, and because I knew father would not be able to keep his face straight much longer by the way the vein in his neck was throbbing. It always did when he held himself in. "You—you conspirators!" I said. "And I was daft enough to fall for it." I sat down and folded my arms. "You both ought to be ashamed of yourselves! I thought it was supposed to be women who were born matchmakers."

We all laughed about it then, and Nigel tactfully went out to put the lights on his car, and took his time about it.

"Father," I protested. "How could you?"

He put one arm around me and held me tight. "It was worth a try," he said. "I'm not getting any younger, Lucy. I'd like new blood in the old firm. But I'd much rather take in a lad who—who'd see that you took over a good interest in it. I've been thinking about making young Enderby an offer—but I didn't want to do that unless—unless he was the one for you, too. There's plenty of time. And then he told me he wanted to ask you to marry him—and we both wanted to know where we stood. So I told him it was his good temper that spoiled his chances. 'Lucy has to have lame ducks,' I told him. 'Can't you be down on your luck, and wipe that smile off your face? She might soften toward you then,' I said." He kissed my cheek. "You're a lot like your mother, you know. She couldn't stand by and see anyone in trouble. And I don't think you could, either."

"Father, you— All right. I forgive you. You very nearly brought if off, too. When you said, 'If he were my son' I was almost ready to say that he was practically your son-in-law, just to get you to help him." I tapped his hand. "It was naughty, because I'd have backed out again afterward."

"You—you do like the lad, don't you, Lucy?"

"Very much," I assured him. "But I'm not thinking about marriage yet. Not for ages."

"No, I suppose not. Well then, I'm not going to think about another partner just yet, either."

When Nigel came back father switched on the television to watch a science program, and I sat between them, thinking my own thoughts. I wished I had made my prepared speech to Nigel, about being platonic friends, before this had happened.

I tried on the way back to the hospital. But he only laughed at me and said, "All right, darling. You're very young. I can wait. But you're very sweet and I love you, Lucy. I shall keep on asking you."

"Not more than once a month," I told him lightly.

"Agreed. I'll ask you again on May 8," he warned me. "It will be a Saturday."

April 11

I HAD a long letter from Peta yesterday. I told her, in my last, what Mr. Hyde had said about her, and that I had formed the opinion that he was missing her badly.

It seems to have amused her.

...not as though he was my type. I don't know what he will say when he hears that I have someone else in view. But I've told him I'll go back to work

when I'm well enough. I shall be happier there,
Lucy. I feel safe in the bank.

I told Noble about it as we made ourselves a cheese
sandwich at break this morning. "I wonder what she
means," I said. "Someone else in view? Who can she
have met since she left here?"

Noble shook her head. "According to Braich-Jones
there isn't a houseman there worth a second glance.
And she can't have seen anyone else. Unless—" She
smiled dreamily to herself. "Yes, that might explain
it!"

"What? Give."

She shook her head. "No. No, it's just a wild idea of
mine. I won't say a word until I'm sure."

"Noble—you are a tease. Is it someone I know?"

"Could be!" She grinned wickedly. "No use probing.
I won't say. Very suitable, if I'm right."

And that was all she would say. I haven't a notion
what she meant. I have written to ask Peta, but maybe
she will be cagey, too.

I ought to have gone home this afternoon, but I
shouldn't have been able to stay very long. And besides,
I'm still a little cross with father for playing such a
schoolboy trick on me.

I also ought to have written up my physiology lecture—but I have no idea what the second half was
about, and to ask Noble for her notes will just give her
another angle for teasing. And from what I know of
Tealbury, she is probably as much at sea as I am. But I
must do something about it before Wednesday, when
the books have to go into Tut's office.

When Buster came to the ward this morning he
winked at me behind Nurse Shunala's back, as he stood
waiting for her to undress the new hernia baby, and as
he left the cubicles afterward he said, "How's Nig?"

square black writing—the full notes of his lecture on the heart. I looked at the envelope again. It was typed. Buster must have borrowed David's notes—with or without permission—after I'd told him about it, I decided.

But about half an hour later, Buster came into the bathroom where I was sorting laundry and said he wanted a clean speculum for the auriscope. While I fished one out of the sterilizer for him I said, ''Thanks most awfully for the notes.''

''Notes? I'm not with you, nurse dear. What notes? Have I been writing to you in my sleep again?''

''Idiot! No—the lecture notes.''

He smacked his hand to his forehead. ''Oh, Lord! I clean forgot. Don't be sarcastic with me, I truly did forget. I'll do something about it at lunchtime, I promise.'' He took the receiver and speculum and nodded. ''I will, really.''

''You mean you didn't leave them in the front office for me?''

''I certainly didn't. Did someone? One of your mates, perhaps?''

''Hardly. They're Dr. Clifford's notes, and no nurse would leave them there. It must have been somebody from the residents' quarters. Or—''

''Or a consultant. Quite.''

''You don't think—''

''It's pretty obvious.''

''But how did he know I wanted them?''

''Presumably if you spent the whole lecture looking perfectly vacant it was obvious that you weren't taking notes. He's a good scout, you know.''

Staff put her head through the door. ''Nurse, again I must remind you. And for you, Dr. Blunt, there is a child needing. You will come, please?''

Buster went.

How is it possible to prevent myself from thinking about David, when he is this kind of person? Yet I must. I am behaving like a girl of fifteen. I finished the laundry humming, "Lord knows I'm not a schoolgirl, I really shouldn't care; Lord knows I'm not a schoolgirl, in the flurry of her first affair...."

Heddle-White came in to disinfect some rubber sheets while I was there, and she said, "You sound happy, Nurse Elliot. It's the first time I've heard you singing at your work."

"No," I said. "It wasn't that kind of singing. I was singing to clarify my thoughts, I think."

"Nonsense," she told me. "People only sing like that when they're happy."

I tied the laundry label on the hamper. "I'll do those sheets for you," I offered. "I think I'm supposed to, actually."

"That's another sign," she said. "Wanting to do extra work. No, I'll do them."

"Then you must be happy, nurse," I suggested. "I've never known anyone who was such a glutton for other people's jobs."

Her pale eyes blinked at me. "But of course I'm happy! I'm doing the work I want to do. Why shouldn't I be happy? I have never had a single unhappy moment since I came here."

I told her she evidently hadn't worked on Ward 2, but it seemed she had. "Sister Heywood-Bence is not happy," she said. "But it is understandable. She's had a very unhappy life."

"I didn't know," I said. "I thought she'd been here for donkey's years."

"Yes. But she was engaged to a surgeon—Dr. Frayle, whose practice Dr. Welby took over, you know. And he died. In her ward—she had Ward 7 then, you see—and it was very hard luck."

"Tough," I said. "What did he die of?"

"He got a general septicemia, from a nick during an operation on a child—a tracheotomy. Diphtheritic membrane on his gloves, and there you are. General strep infection and all the rest of it. He went out like a light."

"That excuses a lot," I said. "I feel I've been uncharitable."

"I expect you have. That's why I told you."

"Thanks." I rolled the sheets as she dried them. "I don't mind people being odd when I know there's a reason."

Heddle-White's pale blue eyes came around to me again. "There's always a reason for what people do," she assured me "Always. Only sometimes it isn't easy to see it. But you have to go on the assumption that there is one, just the same."

Then why does David go about with Haarstein? Because there's a reason, obviously. And that's what I don't want to know.

But at least I have his lecture notes to copy.

April 14

I AM WRITING this at home—it's my night out again. Father saw me with it and said, "Don't leave it behind this time, will you?"

I said I'd try to remember not to. And then I asked him, "Have you seen The Laurels? It's all being painted up. It looks terribly smart—white paint everywhere. Like an old woman with too light powder."

Father laughed. "Not as bad as that, surely. It's a nice house, Lucy. It deserves a coat of paint. Cradock was telling me he had the job of redecorating all the inside, as well. It should be very nice when it's finished. They're using the best materials, I can tell you. And I believe they've begun work on the garden, too.''

"I do hope they're nice people," I said. "You don't know yet?"

"No. I've got an idea it's being done up for a bride to come to, though. New boiler and radiators, solid-fuel stove, the lot. And a new bath and so on.''

"Not before it was time, either," I said. "The old one had about had it. I always fancied I'd like it done out with green tiles and all that.''

"That's what it's getting. I shall be sorry I sold it soon. But I must say this place is cozier when I'm on my own. Maybe when you come home for good we'll think about a house again, if you'd like it. Unless you have a home of your own by then?''

"Now, father," I warned him. "We've already had that out! I've a job to think about. I want to get qualified, thanks.''

But I am a stage further, I suppose. This morning I went to the operating room again, and this time I was not nervous. Besides, theater sister wasn't there, and Greta Braich-Jones was taking the cases. This time I had no baby to hold, and I was able to stand behind Buster at the top of the table and watch. And he was very kind and told me everything that the R.S.O. was doing.

As the incision was made he said, "Now the muscle, see? Now peritoneum—you see that shiny stuff? Now you'll see the gut—there you are.''

I watched fascinatedly as the R.S.O.'s deft fingers sorted out the boy's appendix and clamped and snipped.

"Small, curved, round needle," Buster told me. "Then he'll use a cutting needle for the skin sutures. And bob's your uncle.'' He turned off the taps of the anesthetic machine and pulled his mask down around his neck. "Learned anything?''

"Lots," I said. "Thanks very much."

"I can't think why people faint, can you?" he grinned.

Braich-Jones senior said, "When you've finished talking to the H.P., Nurse Elliot, perhaps you could bring yourself to take this child back to the ward?"

It's a strange thing, whenever I set eyes on him I am in trouble for gossiping. And yet it has never actually been gossip. That's how easily reputations are made and lost in this place. It's quite astonishing how perfectly innocent encounters can be made to sound significant.

Back in the ward, I helped to put the child to bed and then took the charts back to Sister Hawthorn. "Thank you, nurse. What did they do? Was it a true bill?"

I took a deep breath and told her what they had done, from beginning to end, and I don't think I missed much out. She listened with a surprised expression, and she said, "Bravo, nurse!" mildly. "But I only wanted to know whether they had removed his appendix. Still, you did well to remember so much."

I opened my mouth to say, "Dr. Blunt explained it to me," and then I remembered that I already had a name for chatting with the H.P. and decided to keep quiet. You can have too much of a joke.

April 16

TUT GAVE US our books back this afternoon, at our coaching class. "Excellent work, nurse," she told me tersely as she passed mine over. "I don't know how you absorbed so much, but you did, evidently."

She had given me nineteen out of twenty for my book, and I found out afterward that nobody else had more than sixteen. I knew I had cheated, but after all, we were not supposed to do them from memory, but

from our notes, so it was not really cribbing. All th
same, I would have liked to explain, especially to Nobl
and Tealbury.

It was not until we had our books that I remembere
the notes were still in my room. He would want then
back, and I was not sure what to do with them. So a
teatime I fetched them and took them up to the war
with me, so that I could ask Buster.

But he didn't come—or if he did, I didn't see him—
and when we came off duty at half-past eight, I had t
shove them back behind my apron bib again. They wen
up to supper with me and came down again, and the
were still there when I was talking to some of the other
at the common-room doorway before going up to bed.

But then, looking idly through the French windows,
saw his car standing outside. Without stopping to think
I went straight out into the forecourt and walked acros
to his car, intending to put the notes on the seat wher
he would find them. It had not occurred to me that h
would be sitting in it. Nor that Staff Haarstein would b
there with him.

As soon as I saw them I turned tail, but she opene
the window and said, "Nurse Elliot. Come, please."

I went back slowly. "I—I only wanted to give D
Clifford his lecture notes," I explained. Haarstei
looked very attractive in pale ice blue, with soft gray ft
at the neck.

He leaned forward and reached across her, holdin
his hand out. "I hope they helped?"

"It was the kindest thing to do," I said. "I was con
pletely lost, after knocking those papers flying and a
that. I'm terribly grateful."

I thrust the envelope into his hand and flew. I coul
hear Haarstein laughing as I shut the door. She has
high, tinkling laugh that can be heard for a long di
tance, even though it's not very loud.

April 20

SO MUCH HAS HAPPENED during the last four days that it is difficult now to sort it all out. But it was on Saturday evening that father was taken ill.

I had a late pass until eleven because Nigel had arranged to take me to the theater. When I was at the bank I had a season ticket and never missed a production, but this is the first time I have been since Christmas. The show finished early because they did three one-act plays instead of the usual long one, and when we came out I said, "Let's go and see father."

Nigel didn't think this was much of an idea, I could see, but I had one of my hunches, and I believe in playing them.

Father was quite pleased to see us and whisked his papers away so that we could sit around the fire with him. "Getting the roughs out for the Outpatients job," he told Nigel maliciously. "Started on yours yet?"

Nigel said he hadn't but that he had it all in his head, ready to get on paper. "It won't take long," he said. "They only want roughs, don't they, in the first instance?"

"That's all—but even those take time, my lad."

"And you watch your acoustics this time," I said. "O.P.D. echoes like a swimming pool on a Saturday afternoon, as it is. We don't want any more noise."

Nigel pretended to be affronted. "And just how many times have you been in Outpatients?" he wanted to know.

"Once," I confessed. "To fetch a baby up to the ward. But it was noisy enough then."

"You were probably pinching the poor little thing."

Father began to laugh. And then the laughter changed to a strange gurgling sound, and when I turned my head

his face was a livid bluish white, and he seemed not to ▌
breathing properly. His head fell back on the cushi▐
behind him.

"Nigel!" I said, "He's ill!" I felt for his pulse, but ▐
was so faint that I couldn't be sure I had found it. Nig▐
dashed across to the sideboard for brandy, but fath▐
wasn't able to drink it. "And you shouldn't give it ▐
unconscious people," I said. "What on earth shall ▐
do?" I untied his tie and opened his collar, and m▐
fingers were trembling violently.

"You're the nurse. Is it his heart? Does he have a b▐
heart?"

"He never told me so. Nigel—we must get a doct▐
quickly. Call Dr. Sharp."

"What if he isn't in? It's Saturday, and—"

"Look after him," I said. "I'll go." I called D▐
Sharp's number, but there wasn't any reply, and whil▐
listened to the futile ringing at the other end I thumb▐
through the directory. CAL 99026 was David Clifford▐
number. If anyone knew about hearts, he did. I dialed ▐
quickly.

The operator cut in and said, "Is this an emergen▐
call to this number?"

I said it was, and would she please put it throug▐
Please.

"Then I'm transferring it to WYL 3002," she sai▐
"The doctor is taking calls there this evening."

Somehow the number was familiar, but at the time ▐
was too worried to take it in. And then David answere▐
"Clifford here."

"Please come," I said. "I think father's dying. ▐
don't know what to do!" I began to cry with relief ▐
hearing hearing his voice, and I couldn't go on.

He hesitated for a second and then he asked, "Is th▐
you, Lucy? Lucy Elliot?"

"Yes, it's me. I'm at 59 Gatehouse Lane, it's—"

"I'm coming, Lucy. What is it? Some sort of seizure?"

"He—he sort of choked, and now he isn't breathing properly. He's a terrible color."

"Two minutes—I'm quite close." He clicked the telephone down, and I ran back to father. Nigel was holding him in his arms, and he looked dreadful.

"He's breathing," Nigel said. "But only just. Get a blanket or something, Lucy."

"Dr. Clifford's coming," I told him. "He's nearby."

"Clifford? Not Clifford the specialist?"

"Yes. Yes, he's a consultant. He's a heart man." I pulled my own coat around father's shoulders. "Why?"

"Look—you can't go calling up consultants like that! They're not GPs. What did he—"

"He's coming, Nigel. I had to get somebody, didn't I?" I held father's cold fingers in mine, trying to warm them, until we heard a car stop outside and the quick rattle of footsteps.

He came in ahead of Nigel, with his bag in his hand, opening it as he rounded the door, and after one glance at father he got out a syringe case and a phial. "Get his shirt undone, Lucy. I'm going to put this straight into the heart muscle." He filled the syringe quickly, holding it at eye level to tap out the air bubble and then squirted a little into the hearth. "Right?" I held father while he pushed the long needle accurately between his ribs.

He stood back then and watched father's face, and after a minute or so he reached out his stethoscope and knelt down to listen. I had time then to notice that he was wearing quite undoctorish clothes—a roll-neck sweater, old green corduroys and and shabby brown shoes. There was blue paint on his wrist and his hair fell forward over his eyes. He looked very young.

"He'll do now, Lucy. I shall give him another injec-

tion in a moment—some heparin, I think. It was a nea
squeak, you know.'' He looked at me for the first time
''You know what this is?''

I shook by head. ''No. What?''

''A coronary thrombosis—fortunately a mild one
One we seem to be able to clear. Has he ever had thi
before?''

''He never said so. He did say he had a pain in hi
chest and his arm a few months ago—when we wer
moving house. I think it was because he was tired.''

''Yes, effort angina, I expect. He ought to have seen ;
doctor then. Did he? Who is his doctor?''

''Dr. Sharp,'' I said. ''But he wasn't in.''

''Then I shall have to get in touch with him. In th
meantime, I think we must get your father to the hos
pital.''

''St. Timothy's?''

''Of course—you'd prefer it, wouldn't you?''

''Please,'' I said. ''I don't know what I'd have don
without you. It is kind—''

''Nothing of the sort. I'm glad I was so near. Call up
there's a good girl, and tell night sister. I'll take him int·
Ward 2. And if she says there are no beds she must pu
up a camp bed for a home goer. Mr. Robbins can g·
home tomorrow, instead of Monday, tell her.''

I flew to the telephone. After I'd explained to nigh
sister, I said, ''I shall be late coming in, sister. Will it b
all right?''

''Very well, nurse. I'll put your name in the book.''
could hear her scratching away at the other end. The·
she told me, ''The ambulance will come out straigh
away, tell Dr. Clifford.''

''Thank you, sister.''

Nigel and David were talking to one another. I re
alized they hadn't been introduced, and I hurriedly di
the introductions. ''Nigel will take me back after th

ambulance has been," I said, "I suppose I'd better get father's things together. Will you wait, Nigel?"

"No need for that," David interrupted. "You can go in the ambulance with your father, Lucy. And I'll follow by car. Or would you rather come with me?"

"I'll stay with father, thank you," I told him. "He's beginning to look better, isn't he?"

Father opened his eyes, then, and looked at us all standing around him. "What's up? Did I faint?"

David leaned forward. "Yes, rather a bad faint. We think you ought to rest in bed for a while. My name's Clifford. I'm a doctor."

"A doctor?" He blinked, and then closed his eyes again and began to breath more deeply. His cheeks were losing their ghastly pallor, and the blue had gone from his lips.

"Father, Dr. Clifford is one of the consultants from Tim's. Don't try to talk. We're taking you back there for a day or two. There's an ambulance coming. Just relax—you'll be all right."

I felt very giddy, leaning forward over father, and I clutched the arm of the studio couch to keep from falling. I felt David's arm come around my waist, and then everything began to sway, and I simply let it.

CHAPTER SEVEN

April 20 continued

I DON'T REMEMBER the ambulance calling at the apartment for father at all. It seemed hours later when I came up out of the blackness and sat up to find myself in David's car, settled beside him with a woolly rug wrapped around me.

When I moved he turned his head sharply to look at me and then went back to watching the road. "Feeling better, Lucy?" He put his hand firmly over mine for a second. "Warm enough?"

If I had not been before, I was as soon as he touched me. I said, "Yes, I think so. What happened? Where's father?" Leaning forward to peer through the wind shield, I could see that we were not very far from the hospital. "Is he all right?"

"He's gone on in the ambulance. Your friend Enderby went with him. It seemed better for me to bring you with me, as you were feeling shaky."

I lay back again. "I see. It was good of you. Have I—have I messed up your free time? I didn't know what else to do—we had to get somebody quickly."

"You did perfectly right. I was glad to be able to help." Without looking at me he reached around my shoulders and tucked the rug closer to my neck. "Keep warm; it's been quite a shock for you, I expect."

"I was scared stiff. People think nurses automatically know what to do—and I felt helpless."

"That's understandable—you've not had much experience. We must get your father under treatment straight away. I'll get in touch with Dr. Sharp about it tomorrow." He changed gears to take the corner above the main entrance to St. Timothy's, and a moment later the big car swung slowly into the courtyard and stopped by the ambulance entrance. "You'd better wait outside the ward while I fix things, and then you can see him."

It was only then that the thought of "the gorgon" hit me. "That'll be fine tonight," I said. "But what about tomorrow? Sister Heywood-Bence will never let me see him."

The corner of his mouth twitched. "Sister Heywood-Bence's bark is a lot worse than her bite, you know. But it doesn't apply. When I said I'd take your father into Ward 2, I meant 2A, of course. Two's the female side, where Sister Heywood-Bence is. TwoA is smaller, and we don't have a sister-in-charge. At the moment I haven't even a staff: it's being run by a private nurse. Nurse Dale."

"Oh, I know her! She was specialing a child in the children's ward when I first went there."

"That's right. Sister Heywood-Bence is technically in charge, but she doesn't interfere unless she's asked to do so. In any case, I say who may be visited!" He switched off the car lights and came around to open my door for me. "Don't worry, Lucy. He's going to be all right." He took the rug away from my shoulders and helped me out. "We shall do everything we can, and it will be only a matter of rest and medicine—and learning to take life a little more easily."

All the way up to the ward he held my elbow, and the warmth and strength of his fingers poured strength into me, too. I said, "It isn't easy to get father to take life easily, you know. He'll worry about his work. I can see that coming."

"Hasn't he anyone to help him?"

I explained that Mr. Lines was getting old and doddery and that father was considering taking a younger man into the firm. "He'd thought of asking Nigel Enderby," I said.

David flashed me a quick glance. "I see. I wondered what the tie-up was. He's an ex-patient, isn't he?"

I shrugged. "Yes. But then so must a lot of local people be. He lives only around the corner from us. He came to consult father about some plans, in the beginning."

We stopped in the corridor outside Ward 2A, on the opposite side of the flat from Ward 2, and David clicked his tongue. "That reminds me. Plans. Your father wanted to tell you something about his O.P.D. designs."

I nodded. "Yes, he'll be worrying about the roughs going to the committee. I'll go home tomorrow and see about them."

Nigel came softly out of the private ward, and David left us and went inside. I said, "Thanks, Nigel. Is he all right?"

"He's in bed, and he seems comfortable. You'll stay now, will you? Anything I can do for you before I clear off?"

"No, nothing," I told him. And then I looked up again. "Yes—there is. I don't know whether we locked up the apartment properly or left the fire safe or anything. Will you call there on your way home and see that everything's all right?" I fished in my coat pocket for the key. "Do you mind?"

"Of course not!" He stowed the key away and patted his pocket. "I'll do that. I'll be there inside half an hour." He turned away and then looked back. "By the way, oughtn't I to leave a note for Mrs. Mopp?"

"Mrs. Pinson—yes, will you? I'd be so grateful, Nigel. It's awfully good of you." I wanted to cry because everyone was being so kind to me, and my lips trembled. I think Nigel would have leaned toward and kissed me if David had not come out of the ward again at that moment and beckoned me inside.

Father was very pale, but he looked comfortably settled, and he managed to smile at me when Nurse Stockwell had padded out. "Worm's-eye view," he said feebly.

"That's right," I agreed. "And it won't do you any harm to lie and rest, either. You've been burning the candle at both ends a bit too often, haven't you?" I bent over and kissed his cheek. "Don't fret about a thing. I'll let everyone know. And I'll be in to see you tomorrow."

But when I called in at my lunch break on Sunday morning Private Nurse Dale bobbed out to tell me I'd have to call again later. "Dr. Clifford's looking at him just now," she whispered. "Think yourself lucky that *he* turns out on a Sunday! Talk about VIP treatment!"

"I'll go home this afternoon and get his other pajamas and stuff," I told her.

She nodded. "But don't bring a dressing gown or slippers. We won't be able to keep him in bed if you do—he's already been asking when he can get on with some work." She swished back into father's room, and though I waited as long as I dared I didn't see David come out again.

I changed quickly when I got off duty after lunch, and hurried out to catch the bus. There was time to go home and back comfortably if I caught the first one, and I reached the apartment just as Mrs. Pinson was coming out of the front door. Her face cleared when she saw me. "Oh, there you are, Miss Lucy! How is he, the poor soul? Mr. Enderby said he was very ill." Her kind face was screwed up in sympathy. "I am so sorry. Never planned for this, he didn't."

I explained as she followed me back into the sitting room. "Then I'd be best not to get any food in, had I? But I'll come in every day because of the boiler—there's trouble enough without having the pipes frozen. And I've packed all his night things for you—I thought you'd be sure to come for them." She nodded toward the suitcase on the couch. "It's all there, miss."

"Bless you, Mrs. Pinson. You're a treasure." I looked around the sitting room. All the clutter of father's papers seemed to have been cleared away. "Where have you put his plans? There were some he wanted me to collect. He's worrying about them; so I'd better take them."

"Plans, Miss Lucy? Oh—they'd be the ones Mr. Enderby took, would they?"

"Mr. Enderby? But when? I thought he was leaving you a note last night?"

"Oh, he did, miss. But when he come around this morning to bring me your key—here it is." She put it on the table. "And he said he was seeing to the master's things for him—his business papers and that—and he went off with a bundle of them under his arm. I hope I didn't do wrong, Miss Lucy?"

"No—it's all right. I expect father asked him when they were in the ambulance together." I felt hurt that father should have asked Nigel to look after his precious plans. And I couldn't help wondering how Nigel had proposed to get into the house to collect them if I had not offered my key for him to see to the fire.

Nurse Dale was looking out for me when I got back to Ward 2A just before five o'clock. "Go in—he's expecting you," she told me. "But don't stay long, he's very sleepy. He was awfully restless earlier on, and Dr. Blunt ordered him some Amytal. Don't let him talk too much."

He looked very weary and didn't have much color. As soon as I went in and began to stack his belongings in the locker cupboard he said, "Lucy—did you get those roughs for the extensions?"

I patted his arm and smiled up at him. "What makes you think I'd forget?"

"Nothing. But I'd like to get them sent in—then I can relax."

"You can relax now, then," I told him. "It's as good as done."

There was not time to phone Nigel—I had to hurry back to the ward. It was a heavy evening: there were three emergencies for the operating room, and I had to do Tealbury's jobs as well as my own, while she took them up, and make up the beds, too. There was a fat toddler with intussusception, a boy of ten with an acute appendix and a little girl of about seven who had swallowed a tiny perfume bottle. Staff Haarstein showed me the X rays of the last one, and when the ward had calmed down she asked for my crosspaper and gave me ticks for operation beds and for postoperative care of patients. She looked up from the table as she folded the chart into its big blue envelope again. "How is your father, nurse?"

"I don't really know, staff. He seems more like himself, but he looks very tired. How long will it be before he's fit?"

She pondered, playing with the paper knife. "This is difficult to say. Weeks, perhaps. I do not know. You must ask Dr. Clifford, of course. But even he may not be able to tell you with definiteness. He is a very good physician, and hearts are his special work. You are very fortunate."

"Very fortunate," I agreed. And then I said, "I can't think how he happened to be so nearby. It was a dispensation of providence."

As she stood up, Haarstein's face shivered into a laugh like smooth water breaking into ripples at the touch of a leaf. "You cannot? I am surprised, nurse. You of all people!"

"No," I said, "It was just luck. I had no idea he was anywhere around—" And then I thought of the blue paint on David's wrist and the clothes he had been wearing. I remembered the things father had told me, and suddenly it was all most horribly clear. Even the telephone number clicked into place in the jigsaw. I had been an absolute fool.

I just stood there, looking dumbly at Haarstein, not listening to what she was telling me. I only caught the last few words. "It is most beautiful," she said, "Dr. Clifford has very good taste."

"Yes," I said between my teeth. "I'm sure he has, staff." No doubt his taste in houses was like his taste in women, I told myself, as I blundered away into the annex. Blue and white was what you might expect a man to choose who had a thing about a cool, pale blonde. Savagely I promised myself that I would repaint my new bedroom at the apartment as soon as I could make time. I didn't want all that Wedgwood blue anymore. It was not for me—a black-haired tomboy ought to have a gayer background altogether.

I asked Heddle-White what she thought, as we tidied the bathroom together later. "Do people's favorite colors reflect their personalities, do you think?"

She looked at me vaguely. "You mean do people like the colors that harmonize with their personalities? Sometimes, I suppose. But sometimes they like the things they lack, as it were. I mean—I know I'm colorless, and I suppose that's why I'm keen on red. And people who aren't at all peaceful sometimes like blue as much as people who are.''

"Maybe that accounts for me," I nodded. "I used to adore blue. Now I think maybe I need something more stimulating around me.''

Heddle-White turned around to look full at me and stopped scrubbing the bath. "You? You don't need a stimulant! You're far too restless as it is. I'd have thought blue was good therapy for you.''

"Not anymore," I said. I fastened the laundry basket. "I've grown up.''

"You're worried about your father, I expect, aren't you?''

Guiltily I realized I hadn't thought about father for nearly an hour. The Laurels filled my horizon—and everything connected with it.

May 1

IT HARDLY SEEMS a fortnight since father was taken ill. I have called in to see him every day, and I have had no time for diarizing. He is looking much better, and Buster says he will soon be allowed to go somewhere to convalesce. "A comfortable hotel on the coast would be just the thing," he told me.

"Yes," I said. "Only it wouldn't be any fun for him, alone.''

Nurse Dale sniffed. "If you think dear matron is going to allow you leave to go with him, you can think again. You know that's one thing she never will stand for—people having leave to nurse relatives.'' She stopped, and her face was pink. "Still—he's got his own ideas about that. Wants to hire a private nurse, I gather.''

I was surprised. "Father does? But he wouldn't go away with a—stranger.''

Her eyes gleamed. "Who said anything about a strange nurse? You'd better go in and see him, instead of wasting time gossiping out here." She winked at Buster and vanished into the linen room.

Father was very cheerful. There were papers all over the locker and floor, and he was sitting up scribbling. I said, "What's all this I hear about you having a nanny to take you away? You could have knocked me down with a packet of gauze. If I'd suggested it you'd have bitten my hand off! Mind you, I think it's a good scheme, but—"

He grinned. "Did she tell you? Ah, she's a nice lass. Seems her sister runs a private nursing home in Babbacombe—and she's willing to make the journey with me and stay there for the duration. Thinks it'd be a good place for me to go." He took my hand. "What does my favorite daughter think?"

"Does it matter? You've made up your mind, that's obvious. But she's quite nice, I know. Is she free to go, then?"

"Bless me, I know more about this hospital's affairs than you do! Haven't you heard—we've a new staff nurse coming here?"

"Oh? Who?"

"Her name's Thyssen, I'm told. She had a compatriot here, named Haarstein, and she's really coming to replace her, because Haarstein's leaving. Seems Tim's has some agreement with a Norwegian hospital that they'll take one nurse at a time."

"Haarstein's leaving?" I longed to feel surprised, but I couldn't. There was a dead weight of cold acceptance somewhere inside, "Yes, I suppose she will be, before long." I kneeled down again to collect the scattered papers. "What's all this mess?"

"Oh, those—I was showing Dr. Clifford my ideas for the Outpatients extension. He thought they were right

on the beam. He and Blunt have just been in to see me.''
Father looked down sharply. ''Lucy—you did get those
roughs in, didn't you?''

''Father—you know I did.'' I remembered, guiltily,
that I had in fact only phoned Nigel to ask him to see
that they went straight to the Management Committee.
But I'd had his assurance that he would ''see to them.''
And I hadn't seen him or heard from him since, but
that, I supposed, was because I had stayed in with father
on almost every off duty I'd had. ''That's the twentieth
time you've asked me.'' I stacked the papers neatly. ''I
do hope you'll get it.''

''It would be nice, yes. Mind—I shall need some help
with it later, if I do. I don't see Lines managing. And
Clifford says I've to get plenty of rest for the next few
months.''

''When will he let you go to—to Babbacombe?''

''Soon, he says. He wants my advice himself, by the
way. Didn't say what about.''

I turned away. ''Didn't he, father? I must go now.
You have a nap, and don't scribble any more today.''

It was as I was going off duty that I met David in the
front hall. He gave me a look that separated me from
Braich-Jones and came across to me with his smooth
slow stride. He was frowning. ''Lucy—I want a word
with you, if you're not in a hurry.''

Not in too much of a hurry for you, I thought. And
then I repressed the thought firmly and looked up without smiling. ''Yes, sir?''

''Tell me—your father's plans for the O.P.D. extensions did go in, I suppose?''

I felt a little exasperated. Two inquiries in one day
was one too many. ''Of course!''

''Well, we had the lot before the Management Committee last night for approval. There certainly weren't
any with his name on.''

I frowned back at him. "But there must be!"

"Did you send them in yourself?"

I shook my head. "But—don't tell me Nigel Enderby didn't send them in for him. He promised!"

David looked down at his feet and then up at the ceiling. "I didn't say your father's plans weren't in, Lucy," he reminded me. "I said there weren't any with his name on them."

"Oh, well—I would recognize them, if that's all."

"So would I," he told me gently. "He's done so many sketches for me that I know them off by heart. And they're in. But they're not signed."

I couldn't see what he was getting at. "Is that so important?"

He hesitated and made patterns with one toe on the parquet floor before he looked up again. His eyes were very blue and shadowed. "It wouldn't be," he said at last. "If they didn't happen to have Nigel Enderby's name on them."

"Oh, no!" I stared blankly. "Have you—have you told father?"

"Not yet. I hardly think it's advisable. Do you? The trouble is, though, that those are—" He plunged his hands in his pockets. "No, I'm talking out of school."

"You mean they've been chosen?"

"Sorry, Lucy. I can't say any more. But I shall have to look into it. I've more to go on, now that you've told me Enderby made himself responsible for them." He looked at me through his lashes, and my heart leaped up and thudded against my ribs so loudly that I thought he must be able to hear it. "You—you don't mind if this chap lands in a spot of trouble, I take it?"

I came to my senses then. I had almost let my vows go by the board. Somehow I had to fight back against him and against the drowning feeling I had when he looked at me. I had all this out with myself long before, reminded myself. And I was childish enough to want to hit back—hard. I said, "Well, of course I mind! He's—he's asked me to marry him." It was true. "Don't expect me to help to make things awkward for him. I shall have to leave that to you!"

And while he was still staring at me, I walked away very quickly and ran up the stairs. I wanted to kick myself for being so weak, but when I got to my room my eyes were wet.

May 3

I PHONED NIGEL as soon as the telephone was free. He answered himself, eagerly, as though he had been expecting me. "Lucy! How nice! Is everything all right?"

"Father is," I said. "And I suppose I am. But—things aren't. Nigel—those plans of father's. What did you do about them?"

There was a thick silence and then Nigel said, "Do about them? Oh—well, I sent them to the committee, you know. Why?"

"Did you put father's name on them?"

"Oh—I don't know. I can't remember, really. I expect his name was on them wasn't it?"

"Was it?"

Nigel didn't answer for a moment and when he did he lost his temper. "Look, I don't know what all this inquisition's about, but I don't like it. Why all the questions? Anyone would think you suspected me of something from the tone of your voice!"

"Yes," I agreed. "Anyone would. Good night." I slammed the receiver down hard, and home sister stopped to tell me that that was not the way to treat bakelite, and if I knew what I looked like with such an ugly scowl I should very quickly take it off.

But I think I have been wearing it ever since.

This morning Sister Hawthorn called me into the
linen room and stood leaning against the shelves, looking anxious. "Nurse, I didn't want to be unjust—and I
know you've been worried about your father. But he's a
good deal better now, and out of danger, so there's no
excuse. Is there?"

"No excuse, sister? For what?"

She shrugged. "Is your mind so far away from your
work, nurse?" She picked up the temperature book.
"How many of these respirations did you take properly? Look at the charts. As for the sluice room, it's a
disgrace. And I asked you three times yesterday to take
down the dispensary basket—and in the end Nurse Tealbury took it. Not good enough, is it?"

"No, sister. I'm sorry, sister." I kept my hands
behind my back and looked straight ahead, out at the
winter-ragged tennis court, still waiting to be mown.

"But it's no use being sorry, nurse. Is it? Can't you
tell me what's making you so careless? Maybe I could
help, if something's worrying you."

It was no good. The hot tears pricked my eyes until I
couldn't keep them back any longer. I put my head
down on the drawsheet pile and began to sob helplessly.
Inside ten minutes I'd told Sister Hawthorn all there was
to know. She was that kind of person.

When I had finished she pushed me down into her
chair and went out to the kitchen to fetch me a cup
of tea from Ruby's pot. She stood over me while I drank
it.

"Thank you for telling me, nurse. I do understand.
And nothing you said to me will go any further—
promise. I always say linen-room talk is sacred! But you
know, one of the things that seems to be worrying you
simply isn't true."

"Not true, sister?" I stopped mopping my eyes and
looked up at her.

She shook her head. "Not true. Unless you want me to believe that we harbor bigamists at St. Timothy's?"

Tealbury scuffled in from the corridor and looked at sister. "Matron's in the ward," she whispered. "Can you come, sister?" And sister set her cap straight and whisked out, while I began to tidy the linen shelves in case matron came in to see what I was doing there. As I stacked away the sheets and towels, pillow-slips and bandages, I tried to get things into focus.

But lunchtime came before I saw sister alone again, and when I went up I sat next to Noble. "Did you know that Dr. Clifford was married?" I said. She said no she hadn't and turned to ask Braich-Jones before I could stop her.

Braich-Jones swallowed half a bun and shook her head. "Hadn't heard so," she said.

"Something for you to tell Greta," Noble told her. "Nice change!" And then she looked at me. "Who says he is?"

"Sister hinted at it."

Braich-Jones said, "I wonder if his girl friend knows that? I was in Wylde Gren yesterday, and I saw them both coming out of his new house. Very happy together, they were."

"What do you know about his house?" I asked her quickly. Did everyone know all about it except me, I wondered.

Braich-Jones looked at me sidelong and reached for the jar of pickles. "Wake up—you know the other's being demolished."

"How should I know? I don't even know where he lives."

She patiently explained to me that the three big houses that were to make way for the new O.P.D. were his, Dr. Welby's and the house governor's. "They belong to the hospital so they get them at low rent." She

munched her way through another mouthful. "So
they've had to buy new ones, see?"

"Maybe Haarstein's been advising him on decor and
what not," I suggested, more to convince myself than
for Braich-Jones's benefit.

She looked at me narrowly. "Does he strike you as a
man who needs advice? He knows his own mind perfectly well, I'd say. Probably has very definite ideas. No, I
think Haarstein's very much his girl friend—it's darn
funny the way she isn't animated with anyone else, isn't
it?"

She got up to go, and Noble looked across the table
and grinned. "Heard about the O.P.D. extensions?"

"What about them?"

"It's said that Nigel Enderby is designing them. Is it
true?"

I shook my head doubtfully. "I think he entered designs—but so did several other people, including father.
There's no knowing yet. I don't know that the Management Committee has decided on one. They want more
details before they decide—the quantity surveyors
haven't been consulted yet."

"Oh. Somebody said they saw it in the morning
Clarion—pictures and what not."

"Could be," I said. "I must look." I was praying
that Noble was wrong and that if she was right father
hadn't seen the Clarion.

There wasn't a copy in the ward, and I could only get
on with my routine and try to be patient. We got the tea
out early for once, and by the time the porter came up
with his Clarion sticking out of his jacket pocket, I had
only the back tray left to put away before I went off.

He said, "Sure you can have it. There's some picture
of the new O.P.D. on the middle spread, by the way."

"I know," I said. "That's what I wanted it for." I
pushed it wholesale behind my apron bib until I left the

ward and opened it going down the stairs. It was there, right enough. A big "artist's impression" that was clearly taken from father's drawings. Only the caption underneath said, "This is how St. Timothy's extension on Eastbrook Road, will look when it's built to the designs of Mr. Nigel Enderby, the architect of the People's Theatre."

I went straight around to see father. Without stopping to think I flung the *Clarion* on the bed, open at the picture, and burst out, "Look—this is your design, isn't it? We must do something!"

And then I saw his face and raced for Nurse Dale. I stood trembling in the corridor while she sent for hypodermic trays, hot-water bottles and Buster. And when Buster came out of the room again, at last, he took my arm and marched me firmly down the stairs. His face was tight and angry.

"Just what did you think you were up to?"

"I was so furious," I said feebly. "I just didn't think—" I stopped dead on the half landing. "Is he all right? What have I done?"

"You very nearly killed him. Not quite, thank God. Let it be a lesson to you! He'll be all right, I think—but for goodness' sake keep away from him for a day or two, if you can't be trusted not to behave any more sensibly than that. You must be crazy."

I walked stiffly by his side until we came to the ground floor. Then I said, "I'm sorry. Don't be like this—I feel dreadful. I didn't mean to undo all your work."

"It's not my work you've undone, if that's any consolation. It's the chief's. I should think he'll want to strangle you when he hears."

"You mean—you'll tell him?"

Buster shook my hand off his arm. "Tell him? Of course I shall have to tell him. At least I shall have to explain that it was the paper that upset him. And D▮ Clifford will want to know how he got hold of it—afte▮ he'd given careful instructions that your father wasn▮ to see the paper on any account."

"I didn't know—" I wailed.

Someone tapped me on the shoulder, and Buste▮ looked once over my shoulder and hurried on his way "You did know, Lucy," David said. "I told you would look into it. Couldn't you have left it at that? His eyes were like cold steel. "Couldn't you hav▮ trusted me?"

I stared down at my shoes. They looked pretty scruf▮ compared with his beautifully polished pair so firm▮ planted in front of them. I said incoherently, "Pleas▮ Please don't rub it in. I can't bear it—"

I heard him sigh, a long sigh that went right down ▮ his shining shoes and back. And then he gripped my ar▮ and led me quickly into the little waiting room off t▮ hall, where husbands wait for babies to be born a▮ where relatives of patients shed most of their tears.

"Lucy," he said, in a queer shaky voice. "Don'▮ You mustn't cry. I can't bear it, either. Stop it—do y▮ hear!" He pressed my wet face hard against his da▮ gray shoulder and shook me gently. And then he to▮ my cap off, put it down carefully on the table and r▮ his long fingers through my hair. I heard a strange lit▮ laugh before he put his mouth down on mine and kept ▮ there.

After what seemed a long time, he moved his lips ▮ my ear and said, "I'm sorry. I had to stop you." Th▮ he pushed me away from him roughly and marched o▮ The waiting room door slammed shut behind him.

CHAPTER EIGHT

May 4

HOW LONG CAN a person go on feeling shaken after a crisis? When I discussed this once with Peta she said, "Only so long as the crisis lasts—the moment it's over the whole thing gets resolved in the light laugh, you know."

This is one time when Peta's theories don't apply. Because I feel less like a light laugh than I ever felt, if my memory isn't playing tricks. And I feel not only shaken, but disintegrated.

I am still dreadfully worried about father, even though Nurse Dale says he is improving after yesterday's collapse. She says she is not allowed to let me see him yet, but she let me peep through the crack of the door and look at him lying there. They have taken away some of his pillows, and he is a ghastly color. And it is all my fault.

Quite apart from this, I can't help going back to the moment when David took me into the waiting room. It doesn't seem quite real, even now, though I know it must be because where he gripped my arm there is a small, blue bruise, the size of his thumb. But the worst part was that a second after he had left me the door opened again, and Nurse Shunala ushered a couple of parents in. I muttered something and pushed past them in the doorway, and when she had shut them in she looked at me oddly and said, "So? Did you quarrel with Dr. Clifford?"

I rammed my cap into place and tried to look normal. "No. Why do you say that?"

Shunala lifted her hands and dropped them again. "He nearly knocked me down as he came out. He looked most enraged." Her dark eyes came closer. "What did you say to him, hmm?"

I turned away without answering and hurried upstairs to the dining room. But when I got there I found I couldn't eat, and I sat drinking coffee until the last people had gone. Even then I was still trembling, and as I walked across to the home, with my cape huddled around my shoulders, my legs felt like cotton wool. They still do.

It all seems such an unmanageable muddle. Nigel is in trouble over the plans—though even now I can't believe that he would do such a thing. Buster is thoroughly angry with me. And David, David whom I respected utterly right from the beginning, has tumbled down from his pedestal just to stop me crying. He hadn't any other reason for taking me in his arms and making me feel as I do. And where does Haarstein fit into it all?

The thing I can't forgive myself is that all the time, through all the other problems, all I can really think clearly about is David. The touch of his fingers and the tenderness of his lips will be with me until I am old. That is the only thing I am sure about.

May 6

IT HAS BEEN my half day again today, and to my surprise it has been a moderately pleasant one. When I called to peep at father after lunch, Buster was bending over the microscope in Ward 2A's clinical room. I tried to walk past the open door quietly, but his head came up, and he shot out into the corridor. He held out his hand, "Pax?"

I hesitated for a second, and then I saw the boyish smile beginning at the corners of his mouth and relaxed. I put my hand in his. "All right. Pax," I agreed. "It was all my fault."

He grinned openly then, and I think he was relieved. "Good girl!" He stood there swinging his stethoscope uncertainly and then he asked, "What are you doing with your half day?"

"How did you know it was my half day?"

"I have my channels," he said airily. Then he leaned forward and whispered, "Peta told me." His cheeks were pink.

"*Peta*? Peta Royde, you mean?"

Buster nodded. "The same. Your chum, remember?"

"Yes, but—"

"I've news for you. You're visiting her this afternoon. All right?"

"Fine," I nodded. "Only how? It's a long way and—"

He patted my shoulder. "Uncle William will get you there. Fear not. You just be outside the home in about half-an-hour's time. Check?"

"Check," I said. And then I raced over to change.

When I got outside, he was waiting for me, in a brand new sedan. It was a neat little car and hardly what I would have expected from him. "New?" I asked, as he shut my door.

He came around and got in himself. "Yes. You're the first passenger. Like it?"

"It's—awfully respectable, isn't it? And I'll bet you get fifty miles to the gallon, don't you? They're frightfully economical, I'm told. And fast." I settled down comfortably in the seat beside him and watched the traffic.

"I wouldn't know. We haven't done fifty miles together yet. And I can't try her for speed because she isn't broken in yet. As to being respectable, I believe it's the acceptable thing for GPs to look moderately reliable?''

''GPs?'' I echoed. ''You mean you're going into practice?''

He nodded, smiling with satisfaction. ''Right the first time. I've managed to persuade my uncle that he needs an assistant—he's in practice in Solihull, you know—and that's that. I'm going at the end of May. Only three weeks and a bit.''

''I hope you'll be very successful,'' I told him. ''If it's what you want, I'll be glad with you.''

His face sobered. ''It's what I want, all right. I like ordinary folks—the kind you meet in Outpatients. Only it isn't all I want.'' He looked at me for a second and then turned away again. ''That's rather where you come in, Lucy.''

For one mad moment I thought he was going to tell me that I mattered in his scheme of things, and then I pulled myself together. ''Where I come in? You'd better explain.''

''Yes, well, I could have told you all this before. Only I waited until I was pretty sure my future was secure before I even dared to think it to myself. Lucy—I want to marry Peta. I've rather brought you with me to...to put the poison down for me. And hold my hand as it were. You're her oldest friend, and you may be able to egg her on a bit, so to speak.''

''Buster! So it was you, after all? She said—''

''She said what?''

I remembered her letter. ''She said she had 'someone in view' once.''

Buster's face fell. ''Oh, no! It could be some other chap, Lucy. I've never told her how I felt.''

I looked at him curiously. ''How often have you seen her? And how did you get to know her in the first place?

She was only on the wards a day or two before she went off sick."

He had the grace to blush again. "I've seen her three times a week ever since. How did I get to know her? Well—" He laughed reminiscently. "She didn't drop a drum on my head, I can tell you that! But it was almost as bad. Her first day on the ward she was sent up to the operating room with a chart, and she slid across the anesthetic-room floor and landed in my lap."

"She never told me."

"No. I don't suppose she did. It was one of those moments, you know. You must have had them?" He glanced at me inquiringly as he pulled out into the main road and edged his way through the lorries and cars ahead. "No?"

I thought about David and closed my eyes to do it better. "Yes," I admitted. "I have. Only mine never lead to anything."

Buster put one arm across my shoulders and hugged me briefly. "Don't you believe it," he told me comfortingly. "The old arrow strikes where you'd least expect it."

"I'm not a very good shot with a bow," I said. "Neither is my guardian Cupid. But I think nothing of it—I have other things to do. Unlike Peta, I've my training to get through."

"Yes. It's a point. But it won't be a point much longer, I hear. Haven't you seen the new recommendations from the Rushcliffe Committee? That the shortage of recruits might be relieved if they were to take on married girls to train? And that more married nurses should be engaged and allowed to live out?"

"No. It sounds too good to be true. But even then, Buster, also unlike Peta I don't have 'somebody in view,' you see."

"Ah. That makes it more difficult. But is it any help if I tell you that somebody has you in view?"

I thought about Nigel and shivered. "No, not a bit. Where are we? Is it much farther?" I looked determinedly out of the window, and for the rest of the journey we talked solidly about the scenery. It wasn't very exciting scenery but it was better than thinking about my private life.

Peta was alone on the ground-floor balcony, in the pale spring sunshine. She hugged me and beamed at Buster, and said, "Now I have everything."

"Not yet, you haven't," I told her. I glared at Buster, and he went back into the ward and picked up a magazine from the table. "Peta—you said you had somebody in view. Remember? When I told you about Mr. Hyde. Quickly, before Buster comes back. Who did you mean?"

She looked over my shoulder into the ward, and there wasn't any mistaking the expression in her eyes. It was the way I felt when I thought about David, only in her case it was happy. "Thank God," I said. "That's one thing that's gone right this week."

She stared at me. "You don't mean he—Lucy! Has he said anything?"

I gave Buster the all clear. "He'll tell you himself." It was my turn to wander away.

Coming back in the car he said, "Let's celebrate, Lucy. What can we do?" He grinned. "And what do I buy the bridesmaid? I've been told you have to have a very costly gem to mark the occasion."

I smiled wryly. "Do I? Well, Tut's always telling us what a gem of a book *Gray's Anatomy* is. You'd better present me with a copy."

"Huh! Jolly fine that would look in the local rag. 'The bridegroom's gift to the bridesmaid was a copy of *Gray's Anatomy*.' Anyway, I've a battered copy you can have for nothing, if you really want one. And several other tomes I don't see myself needing in general practice. You'd better look through them when I move out."

"Thanks," I said. "That'll be nice. As for celebrating—don't think I'm mad, but I'd like to go back and go to bed."

"What on earth for?" He looked shocked. "Not hit the high spots?"

I shook my head. "Nice of you, but no. I want to grab a bath, and I've my diary to write up and—"

He held up his hand. "All right. Don't go on. You've convinced me, Lucy. If you seriously expect me to believe that you keep a diary, then I've no more to say. It just shows me what a bore I must be, if that's the alternative!"

But I don't think he really minded. Like me, he didn't want to talk—he just wanted time to think.

May 8

THIS MORNING I had a letter from Nigel. I had forgotten his promise, until he reminded me. And even if I'd remembered I should have thought it was washed out, after our telephone conversation about the plans.

But he wrote:

"I said I'd propose again on May 8—remember? This is me doing it. I daren't telephone you, Lucy, after last time. So I thought I'd better write. Now that the mix-up about the plans is cleared up, I expect you feel better. I still want to say the same—I love you, and I want to marry you. Is it yes this time?"

I pushed the letter behind my apron bib and went on thinking about it all morning, until I went to Ward 2A. Nurse Dale said, "He's a lot better. I think it will be all right for you to see him." She smiled. "One thing, that business about the plans is straightened out."

I nodded, but I hadn't any idea what she—or Nigel— meant. That was what I wanted to know.

Father looked much more like himself, and I went in carefully, wondering how to get around to what I had to say. But he said it for me. "My word, you gave me a shock with that newspaper, Lucy! But it's all over now, thank goodness. I expect you've heard?"

"No, father. What happened?"

"Why, they were my plans, of course, and Nigel had omitted to put the covering letter in with them. Of course, they went in with his own, and it was taken for granted they were from the same person. Not the lad's fault, really. Seems he left it to his secretary to enclose a letter, and she left it to him, and that was how it all happened. The newspapers didn't check with him before they printed the thing."

My heart lightened. "I see. So you do get the job?"

"I do. Or rather, Elliot, Lines and Enderby do!" He looked up at me to see how I was going to react. "It is all right between you two young people, isn't it, Lucy? Nigel tells me he wants to marry you, and that he's very anxious to make you happy."

I nodded slowly. And then I looked at father's thin face. "Is it what you want, father?" I knew then that it had to be what he wanted, or it was no good. I owed him so much. And I had nearly killed him. "Do you want me to marry him?"

He nodded and put his hand over mine. "I do. If you think you could be happy with him. He's a good lad, Lucy. And he's a good architect, too. I need him in the business."

"All right, father. Then I'll tell him it's yes, shall I? Only—I don't want to get married yet. I don't want to leave the hospital, really."

"There's no hurry, girlie. You're young yet. But I'd like to see you settled, you know." He smiled again. "Like to see some grandchildren before too long, too!"

I kissed him. "I know. Give me time, father. I'm only twenty."

"Your mother was twenty-two when I married her. It's a lovely age." He closed his eyes and began to doze off, and I left him and went to phone Nigel.

He is coming to take me out tonight, and before he does, I have to get everything straight in my mind. My future is all planned now. I am going to be Mrs. Nigel Enderby, and I suppose father and Nigel and I will all live together. At first, anyway. It seems odd, that everything that was so fluid is so neatly settled, so quickly. Only a couple of days ago I thought things would never sort themselves out. But that was because I was dreaming silly schoolgirl dreams, instead of looking at what was right under my nose. We all have to come down to earth, I suppose, sooner or later.

Nigel will make a very handsome bridegroom. I suppose we shall have at least one red-haired child, like him, with his father's bright curls and impish smile. And I shall settle down into domesticity, as though all this trouble had never been. People do. I expect everyone goes through a period of indecision first. I know now that there is nothing to worry about anymore. It is all mapped out.

May 9

NIGEL WAS VERY SWEET to me last night. He has given me a beautiful ring—a solitaire diamond that must have cost the earth. It is a little loose, and he is going to get it made smaller later on, but just for now I am keeping it as it is. He took me out to dinner at the St. James's, where I went with father, and bought me champagne. I always thought it would be wonderful stuff to taste, but it struck me as being very like cider. But I didn't say so. Nigel would have been hurt.

He is full of plans. He wants us to look for a house and not live at the apartment. He says a successful architect ought to live in a proper house, and it's no use arguing because he's talked about it to father, and father has agreed to come and live with us wherever we choose.

"All right," I said. "But one thing I do insist on—I must have Mrs. Pinson."

"You shall," he promised. "Lucy—you don't really want to stay on at the hospital, do you? Let's get married soon. As soon as your father's well enough to come to church and give you away. Please, darling!"

I don't know whether it was the effect of the half a glass of champagne I'd had or whether it was just that I came to my senses at last, but I said, "No. You're right, Nigel. I want to make a clean break." And I agreed that I'd give matron the usual quarter's notice and hope that father would be well enough for us to be married in September. I knew, all at once, that I had only one reason for wanting to stay at St. Timothy's, and it was a bad one.

I remembered then that I still had to tell the people at the hospital about our engagement. "I suppose we shall have to tell people," I said uncertainly. "Or would you rather not?"

Nigel reached across the table for my hand. "I'm ahead of you, sweet. It's done. There'll be an announcement in the *Clarion* tomorrow. My parents tell me that inserting the announcements is the bride's parents' job, but your father says it's theirs. I don't know. But, in any case, they both gave me carte blanche to go ahead with it."

I frowned. "But *I* didn't," I protested. "You didn't ask me."

Nigel shook his head at me. "Now, Lucy. Let's start as we mean to go on, there's a darling. You're not going to turn into one of those awful bossy women, are you? A man does like a pliable wife, you know. I've not much time for backseat drivers, I'm afraid." He wasn't smiling anymore. I remembered then that his mother is a very dominant sort of woman and that his father is very quiet. I could understand why he was scared.

"No, of course not," I told him. "Only—supposing I'd said no?"

"Darling, I'm not quite without imagination. I waited until you said yes before I sent it in. You don't know how happy it made me to do it, Lucy." He stroked my fingers persuasively. "I know I'm lucky. I want to tell the world. It's only natural, isn't it? So I wanted to announce it straightaway, of course."

"I know," I said. "It's all right." I brightened a little as I thought of the other girls. "I'm longing to see Braich-Jones's face. She won't be able to say 'Greta says' about this."

Nigel groaned. "Oh—that girl! That was my admirer, wasn't it? The one who spun you all those yarns about me?"

I nodded. "But I want to tell Peta first. I want to go and show her my ring." I looked down at the brilliant stone on my finger. "It's a beauty, Nigel."

"Nothing but the best for my girl," he said. "That's how it will always be. You're sweet, Lucy."

He drove me back soon after that and kissed me good-night on the porch of the home. There is no need to hide him anymore. It will all be in the papers tomorrow. Home sister stood in the hall as I went in afterward and said, "Nurse Elliot—please don't make yourself so cheap!"

It gave me a lot of pleasure to flash my ring under her nose and say, "I've just got engaged, sister." Her face was a study.

May 1(

I WENT to matron at nine o'clock this morning. When I asked Sister Hawthorn if I might go she said, "Is it urgent, nurse? Because we have five operating-room cases, and I want you and Nurse Heddle-White to go up alternatively. And we start the list at nine forty-five."

When I said I wanted to hand in my notice, or I'd have to wait until next Monday, her face changed. She looked almost hard. "Very well, nurse. Then Nurse Tealbury can go to the operating room. I'm very sorry to hear this. I thought you were really keen. But if you're leaving, you won't be interested in taking up the splenectomy and the cerebral tumor, will you?"

"Oh, but sister, I wanted to see those done! Can't I—"

"No, nurse. The experience will be more valuable to a nurse who really needs it. Thank you. You may go."

For a moment I almost said, "My notice can wait, sister. Please let me take them up." And then I saw it simply wouldn't be logical. What did a couple of operations more or less matter to me? In three months' time I should be out of it all.

Matron looked startled when I said, "I'd like to give three month's notice, matron. I've put it in writing to the secretary, of course."

"But why, nurse?"

I said, "I'm getting married, matron. In September, I hope."

"Married? But you're very young, nurse. Wouldn't it have been better to finish your training first? You know, your husband may not always be able to keep you—I feel every girl ought to have *some* training before she marries. And besides—this is a mad world, nurse. Trained nurses may be very valuable to the community before much longer, I'm afraid."

I said, "I'm sorry, matron. It's all arranged." And then my imagination took charge. "You see—it's what my father wants. I do think I ought to consider him as he's been so ill."

Matron sat back, and her face closed up like a helianthemum with the sun off it, as though something had died inside her. She could see it was no good. But even then she wouldn't make it easy for me. She fiddled with her big desk calendar and then thudded the lamp up and down a time or two. At last she looked up and said, "Well, nurse, whatever you may say I'm going to give you two weeks to think it over. Until May 24. If you still feel the same then, I'll back date your notice to today. If you change your mind, we'll say no more about it." And that was as far as she would go.

Back in the ward everyone was very busy. Heddle-White and Tealbury were looking after the operation cases, Haarstein was doing treatments, and because Shunala was off duty sister was feeding the babies. I went to her, in the second cubicle, and said, "What would you like me to do, sister?" She didn't answer me at once, and I went on, "Shall I do these feeds for you?"

She slapped down an empty bottle on the locker top, in an impatient way that wasn't at all like her. "No, thank you, nurse. You may clean the sluice room again. It was not done properly before you went to matron, was it? And you can take the dispensary basket down, and the pathology lab specimens, and call at the laundry and ask whether they can send us up some more draw-sheets as soon as possible. When you've done that you can take Harris down to X ray." She didn't look at me at all.

Haarstein was in much the same mood. She doesn't talk much on the ward in any case, but she was even more silent this morning. She only spoke to me once and that was to say, "You will please to take more care with the syringes. The one you have boil, it is cracked. This you must pay for." I hadn't even touched the syringes. She was just assuming, for some reason, that whatever was wrong must be my fault. It was though by giving my notice in I had become an intruder into the nursing world.

I told Braich-Jones about it at lunch. She had already seen the announcement in the *Clarion*. She smiled knowledgeably. "Jealous, my dear," she diagnosed. "These old maids can't bear to think of anyone else getting married. They think you ought to be devoted to the noble profession and all that. You wouldn't catch *me* staying on, in your shoes."

"I shall be so glad to see Nigel tomorrow," I told her. "That's the one great thing about him—he is cheerful. Just what I need after the atmosphere in the children's ward, I can tell you. I think a cheerful husband is going to be a great help to me—I get so depressed when people around me are miserable."

"Oh, yes, he's cheerful all right," Braich-Jones agreed. "Trouble is, those happy-go-lucky people aren't always very reliable. Or at least, that's been my experience."

"Ah, but you haven't had much experience with Nigel, you see," I told her. "He's different."

She looked at me skeptically. "You're probably right. Anyhow, I hope you'll be happy. When's the wedding?"

"I wanted September. But it depends on father, of course. If matron had her way it would be September in three years' time, though. She froze me up, too."

"You'll get used to it. And Sister Hawthorn'll come around. She's never niggly for long."

But even when I came off duty sister showed no signs of softening. Somehow I had to get through to her. I blurted out, when she told me I could go, "Sister—what you said about... about bigamists it doesn't apply anymore. I'm marrying Nigel Enderby, my father's partner."

"Yes, nurse," she said coolly. "So I understand. I read the announcement in the *Clarion*. Is there anything else? I want to finish the report."

May 12

NIGEL DIDN'T take me out yesterday, after all. But it was for a good reason. He said a client had a house to sell at Streetly, and he had arranged to go there on a business matter and look it over at the same time. "You won't want to sit discussing drains, darling," he said. "You'd be bored. Get an early night, and I'll let you know what I think of it. If it's for us, I'll fix up to take you to see it."

But I didn't get an early night, all the same. I went out for dinner with Noble. Father gave me five pounds to celebrate with, and we went to the Grand Hotel and ordered all the things we never get in the hospital. Afterward, over coffee in the lounge, Noble said, "You're a funny girl, Elliot. I never thought you'd do this, you know. I thought you were one of the stayers."

I gave her a warning look. "Don't you give me a matron," I begged. "Haven't I suffered enough?"

She looked at me dreamily. "I'm not lecturing you," she said. "I'm just stating my thoughts. I did think you wouldn't quit. Do you have to? It seems an awful waste."

I shook off all the feelings I no longer have any room

for: I know now that they are only false sentiment. "It's not a waste," I told her. "It's just a job, like anything else, after all. Good Lord, there wasn't all this recrimination when I left the bank! Nobody said, 'You really ought to get your own till before you leave' or told me I was too young to know my own mind."

"No." Noble set her cup down carefully. "But you are, all the same." Her dark eyes flashed unexpectedly. "And I won't take that back so don't ask me to." She looked over my shoulder. "Half the hospital seems to be celebrating something tonight," she remarked. "There's Haarstein and her pal Thyssen."

I turned around as casually as I could. Haarstein was about three tables away with a tall, blond girl very like herself, except that she wore glasses. "So she's arrived? When does Haarstein leave, then?"

Noble shrugged. "This week, maybe. I don't know." She looked up again, and I watched her expression alter, but I couldn't turn around again so soon. She got up. "Shall we go? Getting latish. I want to snatch a bath—I never get time in the mornings."

Curiosity made me look back from the door. There was a tall man in a gray suit sitting with Haarstein and Thyssen. There wasn't much doubt in my mind who it was.

"All right," I said outside. "I saw who was with them. Why didn't you tell me?"

Noble stood stock-still on the pavement and looked at me levelly. "You really want to know? Because I always thought that was the man for you. I still think so. And I shall go on thinking so. Don't say anything—it probably won't be true, if you do. Just keep quiet." She turned and went on walking then, and I didn't say any more until we were on the bus.

I told her, "Nigel's looking at a house tonight. At Streetly. He thinks it may suit us."

"Is he? Then either he looked at it very quickly, or he hasn't gone yet because his car was parked outside the St. James' when we passed it coming in, and it's still there."

"Don't be silly, Noble. It can't be. It must be one like it."

She shrugged. "Could be. But I can't think why it should have the same number. WOV 9892, isn't it? Not that it matters," she added quietly. "I just thought maybe you'd be interested."

Naturally I telephoned Nigel as soon as we got in. He had just arrived, his mother said, and she would call him. I heard her go to the front door and say, "Lucy's on the phone, Nigel," and then he answered me.

"I just got back," he told me. "Thought you'd be in bed."

"I am, nearly. What was it like?"

"What was *what* like?"

"The house, of course," I said. "The one you went to see."

"Oh, that. No it won't do for us, Lucy. It's too small. Only two bedrooms. Very nice, you know—but too tiny altogether. It's a cottage they fixed up."

"I see." I wanted to say that I liked fixed-up cottages and that two bedrooms was all we should need for a time, but I knew he would prefer something larger, so I didn't say anything. Then I said, "Funny, somebody told me your car was in town tonight. It wasn't, was it? Outside the St. James'?"

"In town? No, of course not. Oh—but it may have been. I lent it to a chap from the office. Didn't use it myself. Not guilty."

"I didn't imagine you were," I assured him. "You'd have fetched me if you'd been there."

I went along to Noble's room and told her what he had said. "Fancy asking him," she said. "Haven't you any pride?'' And then she said, ''Sit down. There's something else you ought to know.''

I sat on the end of the bed and waited.

''You remember telling us that Sister Hawthorn had hinted that David Clifford was married?''

I nodded.

''Can you remember exactly what she said?''

''Yes, I think so.'' I hesitated. ''Why do you ask?''

''Never mind that. Tell me exactly what she said.''

I thought back. ''She said that—that it wasn't true that Dr. Clifford and Haarstein were going to get married because we don't harbor bigamists at St. Timothy's.'' I frowned. ''Something like that. Why are you raking it up, anyway?''

She put her hairbrush down with a little bang and looked up at me. ''You poor fish,'' she said. ''Didn't you understand what she meant?''

''Yes, that—''

''No, you didn't! But I know. And since we seem to be saying a lot of things tonight that are better out, I'll tell you, too. Because I've only just found out for certain.''

''Found out what?'' I looked at my hair in her mirror. I knew Nigel wanted me to grow it, and I tried to imagine what it would look like when I did. ''Well?''

Noble lay back on her pillow and folded her arms. ''She wasn't talking about David Clifford at all. She meant Haarstein. It's Haarstein who's married, you idiot.'' She sighed. ''Now go to bed and think that one out.''

I didn't say anything for a minute or two, and then I got up and went over to the window and looked out at the quiet road in the moonlight. ''How do you know?''

''Because I made it my business to find out. And I was told definitely half-an-hour ago, when we came in. She's married to a man who's been in a sanatorium for eleven months. She works to keep him. She gets more money by coming over here because she gets a retainer from her own hospital as well. He's getting better, and soon he'll be home again. That's why she's going back. Got it? Understand now?''

"Yes," I said. "I understand. But you see it isn't my business, is it?'' I closed the door as quietly as I could.

I understand now what Sister Hawthorn meant. That's clear enough. But I still don't understand why Haarstein and David see so much of one another, or why she is so animated with him and so dim with everyone else. It will take more than Noble to explain that away.

Not that I really want to know, except that I see them rather like characters in a book. It would be nice to see some sense in it all.

CHAPTER NINE

FATHER SET OFF for Babbacombe this morning with Nurse Dale. Mrs. Pinson and I went to the station to see them off. We were there when the ambulance from St. Timothy's came in; and we watched the men fit his stretcher into the reserved carriage before we got into the train to say goodbye.

The whistle blew then, and we had to get back on the platform. As we watched the train draw out Mrs. Pinson was crying. "I don't like the looks of him," she kept saying. "I don't like the looks of him at all, that I don't. Oh, miss—I do hope he'll come back all right."

I took her into the nearest espresso bar and bought her some coffee, and after two cups she was less weepy. "You see a big change in him," I said. "It's weeks since you saw him. But he looks so much better than he did. You mustn't worry."

She shook her head in its bright head scarf. "I daresay. But he has just the look of our Graham, Miss Lucy. I don't like it."

She was determined to be miserable, and nothing I said made any difference. In the end I had to leave her and get back to the hospital. As Heddle-White and I served the children's dinners I said, "Mrs. Pinson thought father looked pretty rough. How should he look?"

"It's early days. But he did have two collapses, didn't

he? You can't expect him to be the life and soul of the party yet, can you?''

"I suppose not. But she was going on like Cassandra, prophesying doom right, left and center. I'm worried now." I stationed myself between our two rheumatic fever girls, fed them alternately and tried to think about them instead of father. They are nice kids.

It was the same all day—whatever I was doing I kept hearing Mrs. Pinson's voice saying, "I don't like it, Miss Lucy." So that I was ready for almost any disaster. But when it came, it wasn't what I'd expected.

At supper Nurse Tealbury asked, "Where's Braich-Jones? I've been looking for her all day."

"Holidays," somebody said. "Went last night, didn't she? Gone to Cambria stern and wild, I suppose. It's her brother's twenty-first, or something of the sort."

"That's right," I remembered. "Greta's gone, too, because Shunala has to help in the operating room."

And then Noble came in.

She looked straight at me, came across quickly and put her hand on my shoulder. I began to get up. "Is it father?"

"No. Come outside, will you?"

Out in the corridor she said, "You haven't heard the news?"

"No. What news, Noble?"

"Get hold of yourself, old dear. They're broadcasting for Nigel."

"Broadcasting for him? What do you mean?" I frowned. "You mean he's—wanted?"

"Wanted? That I wouldn't know. He's missing from home, Lucy. Been missing for twenty-fours, apparently. His parents must have gone to the police." She looked at me hard. "Any ideas?"

"No! I don't know what to say. Could he—could he have had an accident?" I sank down on the windowsill behind me. "Why should he be missing? What does it mean?"

Noble examined her fingernails. "He—he couldn't have been in any money troubles, I suppose?"

"I don't think so. He—he always seemed to have plenty. I've never thought about it." I looked up. "There's one thing—"

"If he was short of money it would explain about my ring."

"Where is your ring? You never wear it in the evenings, do you?"

I explained that Nigel had asked for it on Monday because he wanted to get it made smaller.

"That's understandable."

I nodded. "Yes. But he said he would get it done in a day, and that he was taking it to Charlesworth's. Well—I asked them when I went to see father off, and they said it hadn't been brought in yet. Oh, but surely he wouldn't. Do you think that has any bearing?"

Noble folded her arms and leaned against the window beside me. "What I think doesn't matter, lass. The interesting thing to me isn't what Master Enderby had done or not done or what has happened to him. The really interesting thing is your reaction."

"I'm not with you, Noble. How do you mean—my reaction? I can assure you I don't know where Nigel is. I only wish I did."

"No you don't. That's just the point." She took me by the elbows and shook me. "Lucy—you couldn't care less where he is. Could you? Oh, granted, you're concerned, startled and so on. But you don't care. Not really. I see daylight at the end of the tunnel at last." She got up. "Don't stare at me like that. It's true, isn't it?"

"I don't know," I said unsteadily. "I—I shall want notice of that question." I walked up to our bedroom floor with her without saying any more, but when we halted at my door I said, "Noble—I'm all mixed up. I don't know how I feel."

"Can you take any more? Because there's more to come when you're ready."

"I can—I can take anything. What is it?"

She pulled out a newspaper from her apron. "I was scared that the others might have seen it first. "You're prepared for it now." She held it out. "There it is—front page."

I looked at the headlines. "MISSING ARCHITECT SEEN AT AIRPORT," I read. "Nigel Enderby disappears on eve of court proceedings."

I sat down quickly on my bed, and Noble shut the door. "All right, old thing? Take it easy. Want me to give you the gist?"

"No." I shook my head. "I'd better read it." I tried to focus on the swimming print, while she sat quietly beside me. She is a very patient, relaxed person. I suppose her ballet training helps. She will be a very good nurse when she is trained because she is calm.

At last I got the hang of the newspaper item. There was no dodging the fact that Nigel is wanted by the police for money frauds. And among the charges against him is apparently one made by the Hospital Management Committee. "It's that retainer," I told Noble. "I'm sure it must be that. They paid him a hundred guineas, you know. And then they found out the drawings were marked for him in error and asked him to pay it back. And I don't think he got around to it."

"In error, Lucy? Are you sure about those drawings now?"

I looked her in the eye. "I never was. But I had to be loyal, didn't I?"

"Yes. You had to be loyal if you saw it as the right thing. But do you now?"

"I don't know. I just don't know." I remembered

something else then. "Noble—I have to tell matron by
the twenty-fourth whether I want to leave or not."

"Cross that bridge when you come to it. You'll know,
when the time comes." She reached for the paper.
"There's not much more now. But you'd better see it."
She folded it back two pages farther on and tapped a
photograph with her knuckles. "There's this."

It was a photograph of a movie starlet boarding a
plane at London airport. And there was a thick, white
arrow pointing to a man and woman in the background.
There was no need to read the caption underneath. The
faces of the couple were quite clear. They were Nigel
and Braich-Jones.

"I can't believe it," I said at last. "I can believe the
rest. But not that."

"Yet that was the most transparent thing of all,"
Noble commented. "Everybody knew. Look at that
night we went to the Grand—"

"I'm looking at it," I said. "And a lot of other
things."

May 17

I DON'T KNOW WHY I thought that Noble was the
only person likely to behave reasonably. Everybody has
been very kind, unobtrusively making things easier for
me.

When I went on duty this morning, Sister Hawthorn
buttonholed me as soon as she found a chance and took
me into her linen room again. Only this time she was
troubled, not angry. She said, "Nurse—I don't want to
intrude in any way, but I want you to know that I'm so
sorry about all this business. I've been wondering
whether there's anything I can do to make things more
bearable for you—but I hardly think there is."

I looked at the laundry hamper she had half un

packed, and said, "No, sister. There isn't. But thank you, anyhow."

She waved her hand at the muddle. "Would you like to stay in here this morning, and finish this for me? Then, if you like, you can take your half day today, instead of waiting until Thursday."

I knew she was trying to see to it that I didn't have to talk to people any more than I wanted to. "Thank you very much, sister. But isn't it staff's half day?"

She nodded. "It should be. But she leaves on Friday in any case. She's told me she won't mind changing with you—it'll make very little difference to her, now. All right. Finish the shelves for me before lunch, and then you can take up the operating-room case. And at two o'clock you'll be off." She smiled. "By tomorrow things may look better, perhaps."

I steadily plowed my way through the linen, sorting out mending as I went, and at break time I went to my room and stayed there, instead of joining the fight for coffee and bread and cheese.

They had the patient ready for me when I got back to the ward. It was a little girl with a clubfoot who was having her foot manipulated and put in plaster under anesthetic. She knew all the answers: she had gone through it all before, seven times. She didn't expect me to make bright conversation, only to hold her hand. And I was only too glad to have her hold mine, so it worked out pretty comfortably. Dr. Grason-Hinde, the orthopedic surgeon, took a long time over it, and it meant that by the time we went down again sister was off to lunch, with Heddle-White and Tealbury in tow, so that as Shunala had a long morning only Haarstein and I were left on the ward.

I stayed with my girl until she came around, cleaned her mouth, gave her her pillows back, and then I went to finish folding the mending I'd sorted out.

Haarstein was just putting the last nightgown on the pile. She said, "Like to help me with the two o'clock feeds, Nurse Elliot? They are in the heater. If you will please take Baby Reynolds and Baby Todd?"

We settled down in the baby section, with babies on our laps. Sister Hawthorn would only allow them to feed in bed in the most extreme emergency. She said they needed to be cuddled a little, that it meant as much to them as the food in the bottles we were holding.

Haarstein said, "Nurse, I am sorry that you have this trouble. It is so sad. What will you do?" Her pale blue eyes mourned over Baby Fisher's downy head. "It is so very difficult for you."

I shrugged. "What can I do, staff? I'd—I'd given in my notice, and we were to have been married in the autumn. Now—well, I suppose I'll have to call it off."

"You still love this man?" Her head was tilted curiously. "Or do you no longer wish to marry him?"

I put Baby Reynolds up against my shoulder and patted his bubbles up. He crowed and gurgled against my neck, and he smelled of fresh milk and new mown hay. "I just feel that I never want to see him again," I told her frankly. "But maybe that's temporary. I know it's disloyal of me—"

"Not disloyal, no." She tucked up her first baby and unpacked another from his swaddle of blankets. "It is natural. I would not much respect you, nurse, if you did not know that he has done wrong. It is easy to confuse the sin with the sinner."

"How do you mean, staff?"

She sat down again and smiled at her baby. "I mean that one must hate the fault but love the person. That is possible, no?"

I thought about that. Could I hate David, no matter how I might hate anything he did? I knew that I couldn't. But what Nigel had done was gradually becoming part of Nigel. Part of the Nigel I knew and inseparable from him.

Haarstein was looking at me again. "It is possible?"

"No," I said slowly. "It isn't possible."

She nodded briskly. "So. Then you do not love him. Good. You love somebody else."

"Do I?" I was startled. "Do I, staff?"

"Of course." Her voice was so matter-of-fact that I wondered whether she knew what she was saying or how important it was to me. I watched her cuddling Baby Branksome and saw how gently she touched him, and how soft her eyes were when she looked down at him.

I said, "Staff— You're leaving. So it doesn't much matter what I say to you now, does it?"

She was amused. "So long as you are not calling me bad names!" she said. "This will matter!"

"I won't." I paused while I thought it out. "Tell me—are you and Dr. Clifford very good friends?"

I couldn't meet her eyes straight away. When I did look up she was quietly laughing to herself. "Yes, nurse. We are good friends. He has been very kind to me. But I also am being kind to him, with the lessons."

I stared, and gulped. "The—the lessons?"

"Yes, nurse. The language lessons. So good I have taught him, he can now speak with me all the time in Norwegian! That is good, no?"

"That is very good," I agreed dazedly. "You have been teaching him to speak Norwegian? For how long?"

"Since I come here. When I come he know not one word. But now—" Her eyes rolled expressively. "We talk for many hours. Oh, nurse, this is so good! To speak my language with another person in this place! You cannot know. I was very lonely before, but not now."

"And is that why you talk to him so much and go about with him? Is that the only reason?"

She stood up with her baby in her arms and looked down at me where I sat on the low nursing chair, and nodded slowly. "This is the only reason, nurse. What other reason would there be? I am married woman, you know that?"

"Yes. Sister told me." I turned my face away. "I'm sorry—I didn't mean—"

"I hope you did not! No, nurse, Dr. Clifford is very heart-whole, I can tell you. We say heart-whole? Or wholehearted?"

"It depends what you mean. If you say heart-whole you mean he isn't—fond of anyone at all; if you say wholehearted you mean he is very much so, of one special person."

"That is right. Then it is wholehearted that I mean." She went over to the kitchen to reheat her bottle, and when she came back she didn't talk anymore. But I had plenty to think about while I finished with Baby Todd and tucked him back in his cot. More than enough, actually.

As soon as I came off duty I telephoned Nurse Dale. Yes, she said, she had seen the papers, but she hadn't let father know yet. He had settled down nicely, but she wasn't taking any chances.

"Try not to tell him," I said. "Mr. Lines will just have to manage, somehow, for the present."

"Wasn't Mr. Enderby your father's partner?" she wanted to know. "Or did he say the agreement wasn't completed?"

"It wasn't," I told her thankfully. "I'm glad now. If he says anything about that you'll have to say what you think is best."

She laughed. "Don't worry. No patient ever bullied

anything out of me yet. Keep cheerful—things will sort out eventually."

"I'm trying," I said. "I'm going to play golf and see if that helps to get it out of my system."

She said she thought that was a good idea.

I only thought of it, in fact, while I was talking to her. But I shall go all the same. I have stayed in so long with father that fresh air will be a pleasant change.

May 18

THE FIRST PERSON I met at the club was Mr. Hyde. He was messing about on the eighteenth fairway, alone, and waved his brassie at me when he saw me. "Like to give me a game, Lucy? Members are a bit thin on the ground today." He came up and joined me on the first tee. "Nice to see you. How's your father progressing?"

When I had given him all the news about father and Peta, we drove off. I fluffed my drive and thought of David saying, "Take it again." I looked at Mr. Hyde, but he wasn't making any such concessions. I did better with my spoon because I remembered what to do about my left hand.

Along the second, Mr. Hyde began to talk about Peta again. "I wonder whether she'd allow me to give her away, at her wedding?"

"Why, that's a wonderful idea," I said. "Who else is there? Only father—she's always borrowed him, you know—and he won't be well enough to gallivant for some time. Would you?"

He nodded and bent to dig his toe into the turf. "Hope you're teeing up on the fairways, Lucy. You saw the notice? Never get this stuff into condition if people don't help. Yes, of course I'd like to. Only she might not think it suitable."

"Rubbish," I said. "You're her ex-employer. Why not?"

His ball went sailing onto the green. "Indeed. Why not? I want to give her a good present, you know. You might perhaps help me with that. I thought perhaps a dining-room suite, or—"

I was so astonished at his big ideas as to what constituted a good wedding present that I lifted my head too soon and topped my ball, so that it went skimming off at right angles through the hedge to the next fairway. I heard the thud, but I had no idea what it had struck until I pushed through the bushes to retrieve it and found David Clifford kneeling to roll down his partner's sock.

They both turned to look at me, and then David's eyes slid away.

I said, "I'm awfully sorry! I hope it—"

"There's no harm done," David said abruptly. He fingered the blue bruise that was appearing and flushed.

His partner nodded. "Forget it. It was a stinger, but there are no bones broken. Are there, David?"

David stood up. "No. I think you'll live. Shall we get on?" He didn't look at me again at all, and the other man nodded to me again and followed him without saying anything more.

Mr. Hyde had played on, and I had to hurry to catch up with him.

"Who did you damage?" he asked. "Or were you lucky?"

"I wasn't," I said. "I—I don't know who he was. He didn't say much."

He looked at me sharply. "I thought that fellow Clifford was playing along there. Wasn't he?"

"Er, yes, he was. But it was his partner I hit."

"I see. I hear he's moving out Sutton way. Maybe he'll join the club altogether, then."

"Maybe," I said. "Dr. Coombes may be able to persuade him." And then I changed the subject and got him to tell me all about what was going on at the bank. I listened with half an ear and thought about David, and wondered why the very sight of him turned my knees to water, even when he was obviously quite uninterested in me. It was all a matter of chemical reactions, I told myself. It had nothing to do with me or my emotions at all. It was purely a mechanical thing, and there was nothing I could do about it.

Mr. Hyde wanted to give me one of Robert's high teas, but I said I wanted to call at the apartment and see whether Mrs. Pinson needed me for anything, and whether everything was all right there.

"Then I'll drive you over," he said. "I don't want to eat alone, and I ought to do a spot more work before I finish, even if it is my day off."

He dropped me outside the apartment, and though I offered him tea he said, "No, I don't suppose there's much food in stock just now. Let me know about that wedding present, won't you?"

I said I would and stood by the gate to watch him drive away.

The apartment was as tidy as a new pin, but there was nobody there. Mrs. Pinson had banked up the boiler for the night, obviously. I put the kettle on to boil and then realized that though there was plenty of canned food in the house, there was no milk and no bread. I put my coat on again and took a basket with me. The corner shop by the station would still be open, I decided. They never close until after seven.

I didn't need to, but I went around past The Laurels automatically. Cradock, the builder, was coming out of the gate as I passed. He saluted me. "Evening, Miss Elliot. I expect it seems funny not to turn in at this gate."

"It does, Mr. Cradock. Have you finished?"

He looked back over his shoulder at the gleaming new white paint of the front door. "Not quite. Matter of fact, I thought I was going to be able to. The owner decided to put it up for sale again a few days ago!"

"For sale? But why?"

Cradock shrugged. "Said his plans had changed. Seemed very down, too. But it's all right—he came along yesterday and told me he'd decided to keep it after all. For the present, anyway, he said. So I can go ahead and make a job of it." He put down his books and the tools he was carrying on the top of the broad, stone wall. "Tell you what—like to look around miss?"

My heart quickened. And then I said, "Oh, but he might not like it."

"He won't mind, miss. Only natural you should be interested, after all!"

"Why, Mr. Cradock?" I looked at him, bewildered. "Why me?"

"Well, you having lived here so long, miss. That was what I meant."

I knew I was blushing. "Yes, of course. Well—if you think it's all right—"

He opened the gate, and we turned into the driveway. He fished the key out of his trouser pocket and opened the front door. "After you, miss."

It was all so clean and new that it took my breath away.

We had managed with our old kitchen, and it had never seemed anything more than a little shabby. But when I saw the new one I realized what we had put up with. It was like a glossy advertisement, with its big white solid fuel stove, and its double sinks and range of fitted cupboards with a rose pink counter beneath them. "It's beautiful," I said. "Was it very expensive to do?"

Cradock nodded. "Well, yes, it was. But there—he

said, 'I want the very best, Cradock, and I'm ready to pay for it.' So what would you have done?''

"Given him the best," I agreed.

Then he showed me the sitting rooms, with their off-white paneling where I had always known dark-stained wood; the cloakroom that had been made out of the cupboard under the stairs; and the new parquet floor in the hall.

"Come upstairs," he suggested. He looked at his watch. "Oh, my! My missus will be on the warpath. I'd better go. Look, miss—you carry on. You can slam the door behind you when you go. Will you?''

Before I could say anything he was off.

When he had gone, I went slowly up the stairs, loving the familiar feel of the smooth, old wood of the handrail. Cradock hadn't painted that over, I was glad to see. I had been rubbing my hands on that ever since I could remember, since I first learned to reach up for it instead of holding the uprights. And I had slid down it often enough, too, in spite of Mrs. Pinson's efforts to stop me. In the end, father had had a big knob put on the newel post, at the bottom, so that I shouldn't fly straight off and crash into the front door.

Both the middle bedrooms were done in palest gray and lilac—I hardly knew them with the old flowered wallpaper gone. The bathroom was a gleaming expanse of nile-green tiling, with a new bath to match, and a huge mirror covering almost the whole of the end wall.

But when I opened the white door of the big room that had been father's, I found it hadn't been touched. Evidently that was what Cradock still had to do. I closed the door again and went over to my old room, overlooking the garden. I had saved that till last.

For a moment I had the same feeling of shock as I once had in the home, when I'd gone up a floor too high, while daydreaming, and walked into a room that

was the replica of my own but an entirely different col-
or. I stood at the door for a long time before I could
believe it, and then I went slowly inside.

It was a dream of a room. The walls had been painted
with a matsurfaced Wedgwood blue, the exact shade I
love so much and have in my room at the apartment.
The trim was soft bluish white and the ceiling mush-
room pink. But the important thing, the thing that held
me breathless, was that the longest blue wall held the
picture I had promised myself for so long—an off-white
frame, perfectly plain, held Guermacheff's *Lengthening
Shadows*, with its long, sunset pathway between silver
birches and its colors ranging from palest turquoise to
deep purple, diagonally, behind the orange pink glow of
the trees and the snow.

I sat down slowly on the window seat and looked my
fill at it from fifteen feet away. Then I went up closer
and stood drinking it in.

If I hadn't been so staggered, and so absorbed, I
might have heard his footsteps, but in fact I didn't know
that David was in the house until he stood at the bedroom door and said, "Well—will it do?"

I could only stand and look at him, and he looked
back, without smiling.

"Will it do?" he repeated. "Is that the one?"

"The—the one?"

He came over to me then and put his hands on my
shoulders very gently. "The one you wanted, Lucy.
Nobody had heard of it—but I found it in the end.
Young John, up at the Vesey Galleries, knew it right
away, and got it for me. Is it the one?"

I nodded. And then I said stupidly, "But how did you
know?"

"If you *will* leave your diary here— And I had to read
some of it to find out whose it was, you see. I'm only
human, Lucy, and when I saw my own name—"

I had been trembling before, but when he said the word "diary" I began to shake like a leaf, and my face was burning. I wished the floor that Cradock had painted so beautifully would come apart and let me sink down out of sight. Since it showed no signs of obliging, I had to hold onto David's lapels for support. "Come and sit down," he said. "Let me explain."

We sat down side by side on the wide window seat, and he put his arm firmly around my shoulders. "This room is yours, Lucy. I tried to make it the way you wanted. I did every bit myself."

I remembered the blue paint that had been on his wrist when we called him to father.

"It's lovely," I said. "It's perfect."

"I didn't let Cradock touch it at all." He began to stroke my hair with long, rhythmic movements, and I put my head down on his shoulder and let the tears come.

When he had his handkerchief back again he said, "Well—what's to be done about it?"

"About what?" I was twisting the ends of his russet tie into a tight knot.

"About this room, for one thing. I told you, Lucy, it's yours. If you'll accept it. If you want to finish your training as a single woman, I'll get my sister to keep house for me, and this is yours whenever you want to come. If you want to take advantage of the new recommendations, then it's your own private sitting room, right from the beginning. In that case—well, I've left the big room for you to choose the decorations."

I sat bolt upright. "New recommendations? Big room? Me choose the decorations?" I shook my head. "What are you saying?"

"The new recommendations about allowing people in training to be married, of course," he said reasonably. "And naturally you'll want to choose the colors for your own—'' Then he began to laugh. "I'm such a fool," he confessed. "I didn't even ask you, did I?" His face sobered. "Lucy, dear Lucy, is there any chance that you'll ever be able to marry me?"

All I could get out was, "But I'm still engaged to—"

He kissed me then, and nothing else mattered. After a very long time he lifted his head and said, "Dear little goose! Your young man elopes with someone else; you haven't even a ring to show because he's had to return it to the shop that was dunning him for payment on it— yes, I even knew that—and he does his damnedest to defraud your father of several thousand pounds. And then you tell me you still consider yourself engaged to him! I wonder how much you'll let me get away with?"

He pulled me to my feet. "We shall say it all again, Lucy. Often. But just for the record I love you very much. So much that I think I'd have died if you'd really married Enderby. But I kept on hanging onto the thought of all you'd said in the diary and telling myself that you loved me."

"I did," I said. "I do. I always have. I always will. You're all I want, ever. Except—" I began to laugh.

"Except what?"

"Oh—silly things. Father really well—a double wedding with Peta—"

"Hold hard!" David said sharply. "That's out!"

"What?"

"We'll get your father really well, I don't mean that. But the double wedding. No. Definitely no. I'm having you to myself, and you're having no say in the matter at all. This is where I put my foot down for the first and last time, my love. No double weddings." He led me over to the door. "Goose!" he said on the landing. "Don't you see—you won't have all the fun of being Peta's bridesmaid, if you don't let her get married first?"

"Of course," I said. "Darling David, you're so clever. I should never have thought of that." We kissed again on the strength of it.

We went downstairs then, and there was Cradock coming in at the gate because he had seen the front door open and thought I'd forgotten to slam it shut. When David had got rid of him and stowed me in the car he said, "Where are we going?"

I sighed. "The apartment. I left the kettle on, about an hour ago!"

David laughed helplessly, and I joined in. Then he said, "You'll certainly need Mrs. Pinson to look after you when we're married, darling."

"When we're married," I said thoughtfully. "Oh, David!"

He switched off the engine again, turned toward me and opened his arms. They were very comfortable.

June 3rd

I AM going to finish my diary now because after this it won't be mine anymore. It will be ours. We shall begin it on the first day of our honeymoon. Norway sounds wonderful.

HARLEQUIN CLASSIC LIBRARY

Great old romance classics...
Available now for the first time
in paperback since their
original publication!

Don't miss this opportunity to own some of the
finest in romance fiction—best-selling favorites
from our early publishing program.

On the following page are listed the first two
sets of novels in the Harlequin Classic Library.
These very special love stories are available
only through Harlequin Reader Service.

Get 2 books FREE!

If you order all nine novels in the first set,
you will receive a free book—*Meet the Warrens*, a
heartwarming classic romance by Lucy Agnes
Hancock, a popular American writer famous for
her many delightfully intriguing love stories.

If you order, in a single purchase, all nine novels in
the second set, you will receive a second free book
by Lucy Agnes Hancock—*Nurse in White*, an
appealing story of romance within the
walls of a big-city hospital.

HARLEQUIN CLASSIC LIBRARY

Here is the first set of 9 novels in the
Harlequin Classic Library.

Purchase all **9** at one time and
receive ABSOLUTELY FREE
Meet the Warrens, a classic romance
by LUCY AGNES HANCOCK.

1 **Do Something Dangerous** Elizabeth Hoy (501)
2 **Queen's Counsel** Alex Stuart (506)
3 **On the Air** Mary Burchell (521)
4 **Doctor Memsahib** Juliet Shore (531)
5 **Castle in Corsica** Anne Weale (537)
6 **So Dear to My Heart** Susan Barrie (572)
7 **Cameron of Gare** Jean S. MacLeod (586)
8 **Doctor Sara Comes Home** Elizabeth Houghton (594)
9 **Summer Lightning** Jill Tahourdin (615)

HARLEQUIN CLASSIC LIBRARY

Here is the second set of 9 novels in the
Harlequin Classic Library.

Purchase all **9** at one time and receive your FREE
book *Nurse in White*, another heartwarming
romance by LUCY AGNES HANCOCK.

10 **When You Have Found Me** Elizabeth Hoy (526)
11 **Return to Love** Alex Stuart (527)
12 **The House of Seven Fountains** Anne Weale (553)
13 **Paris—and My Love** Mary Burchell (565)
14 **Dear Tiberius** Susan Barrie (580)
15 **Sandflower** Jane Arbor (576)
16 **Wednesday's Children** Joyce Dingwell (626)
17 **The Way in the Dark** Jean S. MacLeod (541)
18 **Wintersbride** Sara Seale (560)

(The numbers in brackets are the original Harlequin Romance
book numbers.)

USE COMBINATION ORDER FORM ON THE FOLLOWING PAGE.

HARLEQUIN CLASSIC LIBRARY
Complete and mail order form today!

Harlequin Reader Service

In U.S.A.
MPO Box 707
Niagara Falls, NY 14302

In Canada
649 Ontario St.
Stratford, Ontario N5A 6W2

First Set

☐ 1 ☐ 2 ☐ 3 ☐ 4 ☐ 5 ☐ 6 ☐ 7 ☐ 8 ☐ 9

Number of novels checked _____ × $1.25 = $ _____

BONUS OFFER—Purchase all 9 Harlequin Classic novels at one time and receive your FREE book *Meet the Warrens*.

☐ Yes, I have just purchased all 9 of the above. Please send my FREE copy of *Meet the Warrens*.

Second Set

☐ 10 ☐ 11 ☐ 12 ☐ 13 ☐ 14 ☐ 15 ☐ 16 ☐ 17 ☐ 18

Number of novels checked _____ × $1.25 = $ _____

BONUS OFFER—Purchase all 9 Harlequin Classic novels at one time and receive your FREE book *Nurse in White*.

☐ Yes, I have just purchased all 9 of the above. Please send my FREE copy of *Nurse in White*.

New York State residents please   total $ _____
add appropriate sales tax $ _____

Postage and handling $ _____ .59

                          TOTAL AMOUNT $ _____

I enclose $ _____
(Please send check or money order. We cannot be responsible for cash sent through the mail.)
Prices subject to change without notice.

Name _____
                                    (Please Print)
Address _____

City _____

State/Prov. _____ Zip/Postal Code _____

Offer expires November 30, 1980   005566876